BOOKS

Simply Learning, Simply Best

Simply Learning, Simply Best

倍斯特出版事業有限公司
Best Publishing Ltd.

THE KEY TO SUCCESS IN
FLIGHT ATTENDANT INTERVIEWS!

蔡靈靈 ◎ 著

王牌空服員
100%應試秘笈

飛上青空，實現夢想！ Let Me Show You How！

應試前Your To-Do List

✔了解各家航空公司特色、招募廣告如何看與注意重點
✔打造出眾又符合公司特質的英文自薦信、履歷與自傳
✔充分準備中英文自我介紹、預測英文面試會問些什麼
✔正確朗讀廣播詞、熟記航空相關英文辭彙與重要句型

由三大面向【應試前準備】、【應試技巧】、【飛上青空實境模擬】，提供完整的空服應試資訊，
Hold the key to making your dreams come true!

強力推薦給：
● 空服員求職新鮮人　● 有相關工作經驗，要轉換跑道的在職人士
● 各航空系師生　● 更適合無相關工作經驗，要一圓空服夢的你

MP3

專業美籍老師錄製

作者序

在閱讀本書前，先恭喜自己在年輕時就找到人生目標。

在我大四即將畢業那年，因為好友想當空服員，所以就一起去應考。當時在坊間已經有所謂的空姐補習班，但並未有談論應試密笈這類書籍。

當時我不像各位很早就知道自己的人生目標，因為抱著陪考的心態，所以不想花大錢參加空姐補習班，但既然要考，也希望能考上，所以很認真的自我揣摩，想像考試狀況和應考內容，很幸運地在畢業時馬上進入航空公司培訓，三個月後成為空服員。

你會拿起本書，想必是有心要成為一位空服員。無論你是想參加空服員補習班，或是想藉由書籍了解應考秘笈，請給自己和我十分鐘，先看完本書大綱，大致了解如何選擇航空公司到整個面試流程，並翻到第 144～145 頁有關中英文自我介紹略讀，在這裡，我舉了六個不同的介紹方式和中英文範例和大家分享，就是希望讀者能脫離制式化匠氣的應答，找出只屬於自己的獨特面談方式。由於空服員是需要面對各種不同人、不同狀況的工作，所以應變力和獨立思考能力是非常重要的，若你能讓主考官聽到與眾不同的回答時，肯定能讓他對你印象深刻。

身為過來人的我想與大家分享的是，空服員是個高度服務的行業，無論你外型多亮眼優秀，內在的涵養和性格才是致勝關鍵，對自我的要求和努力也是必要的。

希望各位都能如願成功進入夢想的航空界。

蔡靈靈

Editor's Words

編者序

在企劃《王牌空服員 100% 應試秘笈》初期，我們仔細研究過自家的書籍，發現已出版的《航空英語會話》、《Fantastic Flight空服地勤100%：應試＋工作英語》和《Ground Crew English 航空地勤職場口語英文》這三本書籍較偏向航空業的實務應用面，如何準備應試的部分比重較低；但另外也考量到實務部份的確也和空服應試有關，於是將本書定調為著重應事前準備、應試技巧，但順利錄取培訓後，也能將書籍內容學以致用，於是決定收錄常見於機場與登機前後的廣播詞，幫助考生提前準備，並應用到職場上。

企劃架構確立後，我們花了不少時間挑選作者，也很幸運地找到蔡靈靈老師，她不僅有擔任空服員的經驗，也在精品業界做了多年的教育訓練，這兩個產業都相當重視客戶服務與滿意度，因此她更能從客戶的角度，了解如何提供最完善的服務，而這也正是航空業最注重的項目之一。在撰寫過程中，我們和作者有過密切地來回討論，這都是為了要和網路資源、其他出版物或空服補習班做出更明顯的區隔，也是製作本書的挑戰之一，最後我們以兩大重點做為區隔方針，那就是「有系統」與「即刻提升面試英語能力」。於「有系統」上，考生可透過本書，循序漸進從了解航空業開始，進而了解英文招募廣告的閱讀重點、學會寫出最適合自己與航空公司的自薦信、中英文自傳與履歷，最後進入到中文自我介紹、英文面試的簡答技巧與廣播詞朗讀，讓準備考試可以更有方向；於「即刻提升面試英語能力」上，本書的題庫整理清楚，考生可直接邊「聽」，邊「思考」、「準備」最適合個人特色的答案，同時又能符合應徵公司的要求，在準備考試上，更能事半功倍。

最後，還是要感謝蔡靈靈老師的用心與熱忱，本書終於順利完成，相信本書能嘉惠更多考生，幫助他們一圓飛上青空的夢想！

編輯部

review

導讀

　　在談好寫這本書時，覺得寫這本書對我而言應該非常得心應手，因為自己除了真正擔任過空服員，知道空服員需要的特質和實際工作狀況外，又因為工作關係，有許多搭乘長程飛機出差經驗，所以又能以乘客立場來了解航空公司現在想要找的、能使乘客滿意的空服員。加上離開空服員後的工作領域是奢華產業的教育訓練，所以在看服務與事情的角度上相對要求高，覺得自己能很快地寫完這本書。

　　但在寫作過程中，發現知易行難，很多想像簡單的事，一旦著手去做，原來困難許多。所以想與大家分享，無論你覺得一件事情簡單或困難，最重要的就是立刻去做。想成為一位空服員，就馬上開始行動，機會永遠是留給準備好的人，而且是立刻就行動的人。

　　現在有許多空服員補習班，從外在妝髮到答題技巧都幫各位細心規劃打造，所以我在撰寫本書時，一直不斷思考這本書的存在價值。在研究坊間空姐補習班、空服應考書籍、空服員部落格及網路資料後，我找到這本書的存在價值。

　　在本書中，我希望以引導的方式讓讀者找出只屬於自己的獨特面談方式，尤其希望大家能脫離制式化匠氣的應答。因為空服員是個每天需要面對各種不同人、不同狀況的工作，所以應變力和獨立思考能力是非常重要的，若你能讓主考官聽到與眾不同的回答，肯定能讓他對你印象深刻。

　　但是該如何跟隨引導方式來找出屬於自己的獨特應答呢？以本書第

126-127 頁如何撰寫中英文自傳為例，你會發現我在寫範例前，先分享了引導公式，如中文方面：獨立（性格特質描述）─自助旅行經歷（性格特質舉證）；英文方面：Independent（性格特質描述）- Travelling experiences（性格特質舉證），幫助讀者試著撰寫自我特質同時，還能舉出可應用於未來空服工作的特點。

希望大家在參考範例後，於撰寫時，還是要以上述引導公式想想自己的實際情況，因為只有說出你自己經歷過的人生實際經驗，才不需要死背、才能讓人感受到你的真誠和生命力，讓看你自傳的人覺得是在看一個引人入勝的故事，而不是一份交差的自傳。

還有一點很重要的，那就是其實死背答案是很困難的，只要忘了一句，腦中就會變得一片空白。所以在本書中，除了以引導的方式帶領大家走向空服員之路，還有一個很重要的部分，就是幫你建立心態。

相信我，只要心態正確堅定，什麼樣的面試方式、什麼樣艱難的問題，都難不倒你。

想要追逐空服夢，這一秒就立刻行動吧！

使用 Instructions 說明

以下列出幾個在履歷及自傳當中常會用到的字彙及例句，可以多加利用在履歷自傳上的撰寫。

1. attain **vt** 獲得、達到、完成
- I believe my painstaking to attain my goal in life is worthy.
  我相信我為了達成人生目標所付出的心力是值得的。
- I attain the honor of County Executive Award when I graduated from the elementary school.
  我在小學畢業時，獲得了縣長獎的榮譽。

2. achieve **vt** 實現、達成
- I believe that working hard will achieve my goal.
  ⋯就能達成目標。
- ⋯achieve all my objectives in my life.
  ⋯成我人生中所有目標。

⋯ 完成
⋯ may accomplish.

① 撰寫英文履歷前的最佳參考字彙：懂得活用單字，才能讓履歷寫得更活潑！

② 面試前，快速瀏覽航空英文辭彙與重要句型，快速進入備考狀態！

A

● arrival 入境
We are waiting for the arrival of the next flight.
我們在等下一班入境航班。

● Animal & Plant Quarantine 動植物檢疫
If you bring your dog to Korea, you must submit a healthy certificate to the animal quarantine office the port of entry.
如果你要帶你的小狗去韓國，你必須在入韓⋯⋯將小狗⋯健康證明交給動物檢疫人員。

● airsick 暈機／airsickness Bag 嘔吐袋
If you are prone to get airsick, please take ⋯ you.
如果您會暈機，請隨時帶著嘔吐袋。

● aisle seat 走道座位
Could I have an aisle seat, please?
請給我走道座位。

③ 以字母分類，查找方便快速！

④ 透過性格特質描述練習，撰寫具有自我風格的自傳！

下列的履歷範例是無論男女、無論你所〔□〕業都適用的。你會發現這些範例和其它你〔□〕語或中文自傳必寫句子不同，我是以引導〔□〕己、與眾不同的履歷與自傳。

所以請你在看第 126～135 頁的範例時，想著套色字的重點，例如：

心胸開闊（性格特質描述）

和各國人士交談，接受各種不同文化差異（性格特質舉證）

在美式餐廳工作期間，因為自己在世界各地自助旅行訓練的英語能力與實際了解旅遊地人們的生活，所以許多來台工作或旅遊的外國人會為了來找我交談，特地來我們餐廳用餐。我會和他們分享一些關於台灣文化或旅遊的資訊和經驗，我常想這些和不同國籍人們分享的經驗，是我以後成為空服員與旅客相處的寶貴素材。（以實例強調自己的英語能力與世界觀，同時能應用於未來工作特點）

備註 切記描述後的舉證更重要。同時你人生中的實際經驗，才能讓你的自傳真實有生命力，能讓人像在看一個引人入勝的故事，而不是一份交差的自傳。

⑤ 除了「無工作經驗」的自傳範例外，也有「相關工作經驗」的範例，考生能多方參考。

中文自傳範例 1——無工作經驗

　　蔡靈靈，今年剛從輔仁大學大眾傳播系畢業，評估自身的個性與能力後，選擇空服員為人生另一階段的開始。

　　樂於與人接觸的我（性格特質描述），從小跟家裡附近的商店都很熟，常常買東西變成幫老闆看店做生意，到現在也依然如此。對我而言，人不分親疏遠近，一樣用真誠對待。買舞鞋時看到老闆娘的孩子嘴破，我會馬上介紹自己常用藥給老闆娘，並分享嘴破的治療方法。（性格特質舉證）

空服員性格特質練習中文範例

獨立（性格特質描述）—自助旅行經歷（性格特質舉證）
細心（性格特質描述）—跟朋友用餐幫忙準備餐具面紙（性格特質舉證）
應變能力（性格特質描述）—水打翻了馬上處理（性格特質舉證）

　　在學期間，我在校⋯⋯結識來自各個國家的朋友，以英語跟大家相處交⋯⋯他不同文化，跟不同文化背景的人都能輕鬆應對。⋯⋯語能力與世界觀，同時能應用於未來工作特點）

⑥ 除了有中文範例外，也有英文範例，條列式呈現，有助快速吸收。現在就馬上翻開 3.6 單元吧！

⋯⋯間，每年策畫與籌備與不同大專院校的攝影展活⋯⋯合作，使我學習到更多溝通方式，同時能很快與人⋯⋯己的社團經驗，同時能應用於未來工作特點）

　　感謝您寶貴的時間，祝您今日愉快！

⑦ 英文自我介紹用「聽」的，提升學習效果！

chapter **4** **面試**
❷ 中英文自我介紹範

⑧ 每一範例前皆有說明，點出介紹重點！

範例一

Track 01

介紹姓名、學歷、為什麼能成為一位好的空服員，是安全且一般應試考生會採用的方式。簡潔有重點，容易複製，但較無法令留下深刻印象。

Good morning. Everyone.

My Chinese Name is Tsai Ling Ling. You can call me Lillian. I just graduated from Fu Jen Catholic University. My major is Mass Communication.

I am here because I have confidence to be a great flight attendant. I am outgoing and independent, enjoying communicating with different people. When I was in the university, I joined the English Club and had friends from allover the

大家好，我是蔡靈靈。剛從輔仁大學大眾傳播系畢業。

今天會來參加面試是因為我有自信能成為一個好的空服員。我個性外向獨立，

⑨ 範文內容中英對照，容易學習、閱讀！

chapter 5 面試題庫整理

❺ 關於台灣

答題重點

在應試前，建議以台灣推廣者或是以台灣旅行者的心態了解台灣。無論是台灣景點、文化、交通、當紅的旅遊方式、知名餐廳、著名小吃。由於範圍很廣，資訊很多，所以建議大家在各個分類上，選擇自己有興趣的深入研究，並在答題時強調自己是個喜歡分享的人，分享自己喜愛的事總是會更吸引人。

實用英文句型

◎ 我建議…

例 我建議你更新你的履歷。

I recommend / suggest/propose that you update your resume.

I recommend / suggest/propose your updating your resume

I recommend / suggest/propose that you update your resume

I recommend / suggest/propose you update your resume

◎ 在此介紹的是在這個答題分類中，會常使用到的 if 句型

如果我是……

例 如果我是旅客的導遊，我會建議他參觀故宮博物院。

If I am a tour guide for the passage, I will recommend him visiting the National Pala

⑬　每一題搭配專業美籍老師錄音，題庫答案用「聽」的，準備考試更有效率！

● 注意重點
If 條件句中，if 後面的動詞絕對不會用到 will 這個未來式動詞。

Q1
Track 31

Recommend a Taipei one-day tour (including meals) to a couple on a flight.
推薦機上情侶台北一日遊（包括餐點）。

A1 If I don't take their previous travel experiences to Taipei and their preferences into consideration, I will share my favorite MRT one-day tour. First of all, I will recommend MRT Donmen Station. They can enjoy the atmosphere of Yongkang street, and go to taste the food at the Michelin One-Star restaurant–Din Tai Fung. I personally recommend Pork XiaoLong Bao, House Steamed Chicken Soup, Shrimp Fried Rice and Mini Red Bean Buns. Then they can go to MRT Danshui station to eat famous Oily Bean Curd (Ah Gei), visit Fort Santo Domingo, take a boat to Bali to ride bicycles, and drop by the Shihsanghang Museum of Archaeology. When the night comes, they can go to MRT Xinbeitou station, choosing one of hot spring hotels to enjoy dinner and hot spring to end their day.

如果在不考慮這對情侶是第幾次到台北，有沒有特別偏好之類的，我會分享我自己喜愛的捷運一日遊。首先是捷運東門站的永康街，永康街除了世界知名的米其林一星鼎泰豐本店外，附近店家氛圍也是外國人很喜愛的。到了鼎泰豐，除了小籠包之外，蝦仁蛋炒飯、雞湯和迷你豆沙包也是不能錯過的。之後到淡水捷運站逛淡水老街，去紅毛城、吃阿給，然後搭船到八里騎自行車，順道去十三行博物館。晚上到新北投捷運站的溫泉飯店吃溫泉晚餐，泡溫泉，結束美好的一天。

1 應試前進備

2 應試技巧

3 飛上青空情境大模擬

CONTENTS 目次

✈ ● PART 1 應試前準備

PART 2 應試技巧

PART 1 應試前準備

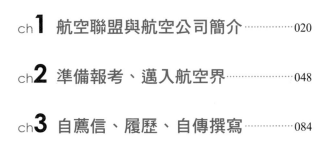

chapter 1 航空聯盟與航空公司簡介
❶ 航空界現況

　　目前航空業界由於廉航的加入，使航空公司家數增加，相對的對空服員的需求也上揚。在你／妳選擇航空公司時，除了應試時間可參考外，航空公司的規模、薪資結構、福利與居住地點也是非常重要的。

　　目前航空界約有 240 家航空公司，其中約 60 家航空公司為了能資源共享而互相結盟。現有三大航空聯盟，分別為天合聯盟（Sky Team, ST）、星空聯盟（Star Alliance, SA）及寰宇一家（OneWorld, OW）

天合聯盟（Sky Team, ST）

　　網址：www.skyteam.com

　　全球性的航空聯盟，現有 20 家航空公司成員，飛往全球 1,052 個目的地。天合聯盟是在 2000 年 6 月，由墨西哥國際航空、法航、達美航空與大韓航空組成。目前的 20 家航空成員為：

俄羅斯國際航空公司（Aeroflot）	阿根廷航空公司（Aerolineas）
墨西哥航空公司 （Aeromexico）	西班牙歐洲航空公司 （Air Europa）
法國航空公司（Air France）	義大利航空公司（Alitalia）
中華航空公司 （China Airlines）	中國東方航空公司 （China Eastern Airlines）
中國南方航空公司 （China Southern Airlines）	捷克航空公司 （Czech Airlines)

達美航空公司 （Delta Air Lines)	印尼鷹航空公司 （Garuda Indonesia)
肯亞航空公司（Kenya Airways)	荷蘭皇家航空公司（KLM)
中國南方航空公司 （China Southern Airlines）	捷克航空公司 （Czech Airlines）
達美航空公司 （Delta Air Lines）	印尼鷹航空公司 （Garuda Indonesia）
肯亞航空公司（Kenya Airways）	荷蘭皇家航空公司（KLM）
韓國大韓航空公司（Korean Air）	黎巴嫩中東航空公司（MEA）
沙烏地阿拉伯航空公司（Saudia）	羅馬尼亞航空公司（Tarom）
越南航空公司（Vietnam Airlines）	廈門航空公司（Xiamen Airlines）

星空聯盟（Star Alliance, SA）

網址：www.staralliance.com

全球性的航空聯盟，由 5 家航空公司創立於 1997 年，現有 27 家航空公司成員，飛往全球 175 個國家，1,077 個航點。目前的 27 家航空成員為：

亞德里亞航空（Adria Airways）	愛琴航空（Aegean Airlines）
加拿大航空（Air Canada）	中國國際航空（Air China）
印度航空（Air India）	紐西蘭航空（Air New Zealand）
全日空（ANA）	韓亞航空（Asiana Airlines）
奧地利航空（Austrian）	哥倫比亞航空（Avianca）
布魯塞爾航空（Brussels Airlines）	巴拿馬航空（Copa Airlines）

克羅埃西亞航空（Croatia Airlines）	埃及航空（Egyptair）
埃塞俄比亞航空 （Ethiopian Airlines）	長榮航空（EVA Air）－基地台灣
波蘭航空（LOT Polish Airlines）	德國漢莎航空（Lufthansa）
北歐航空（Scandinavian Airlines）	深圳航空（Shenzhen Airlines）
新加坡航空（Singapore Airlines）	南非航空（South African Airways）
瑞士航空（Swiss）	葡萄牙航空（TAP Portugal）
泰國航空（THAI）－基地泰國	土耳其航空（Turkish Airlines）
聯合航空（United）	

寰宇一家（Oneworld, OW）

網址：www.oneworld.com

全球性的航空聯盟，官方網頁新聞與信息以英文為主，一些基本資訊有簡體中文可供選擇，尚未提供繁體中文介紹。

此聯盟於 1999 年成立，目前由 15 家成員航空公司及 24 家聯屬成員航空公司。現來往於世界 152 個國家，994 個航站。成員航空公司：

柏林航空（airberlin）	國泰航空（Cathay Pacific）
日本航空（Japan Airlines）	馬來西亞航空（Malaysia Airlines）
皇家約旦航空（Royal Jordanian）	oneworld 同盟航空公司 （oneworld airline affiliates）
美國航空（American Airlines）	芬蘭航空（Finnair）

智利國家航空（LAN ）	澳洲航空（Qantas）
S7 航空（S7 Airlines）	英國航空（British Airways）
西班牙國家航空（Iberia）	巴西天馬航空（TAM Airlines）
卡達航空（Qatar Airways）	斯里蘭卡航空（SriLankan Airlines）

memo

1 應試前準備

2 應試技巧

3 飛上青空情境大模擬

前輩經驗巧巧說

在面試時主考官問，你對我們公司了解多少？為什麼想要進入我們公司？這樣類型的問題是常見的，畢竟這是主考官了解面試者對公司的熱愛和忠誠度，尤其亞洲航空公司特別會問這類型的問題。但阿聯酋航空也曾問過這樣的問題，還有可能問兩家航空公司的比較。所以無論你要報考哪家航空公司，公司介紹這個部份是一定要準備的。

關於航空公司介紹，無論是透過航空公司官方網站、發行期刊、新聞發佈消息、網路等，都能找到非常大量的資訊。但困難之處在於，你如何消化吸收這些資訊，並結合自己的想法，讓主考官感受到你不僅熱愛空服員這個工作，更希望能為這間公司效力，與其給主考官一些在網站上就能找到的資訊，不如想想如何在極短的時間內給主考官除了你之外，沒人能想得出的的答案。

在這個大章節中，將為大家將台灣航空公司龐大的資訊量整理成制式資訊供各位參考，包括官方網站、成立期間、航點、會員制度、航空旅遊等等，同時並舉例出航空公司的宣傳點。但在答題時，請一定要加入自己的想法與對公司的熱愛，所以請大家一定要找出自己對報考公司最有感覺的部分，才能讓主考官感受到你發自內心的熱忱，在 **234-235** 頁有範例給大家參考，請大家選好自己有感覺與有把握的介紹點，參考範例寫法，例如：若你對平日對環保特別有意識，就可以此作為介紹內容，如此一定能說出令人驚艷的回答。想起來好像很難對吧？我在開始想要寫航空公司介紹時，心裡也覺得好像沒什麼可寫的。但真正開始動筆後，發現能寫的部分還真多。所以只要你在紙上寫下那個點，而不是在腦中空想，一定能

寫出屬於你自己很棒的航空公司介紹。以下的重點介紹內容不僅能用於關於公司介紹的面試題目中，事實上，許多題型你都能加入你有感覺的公司介紹，甚至你的自我介紹中也能加入你對航空公司有感覺的部分，讓主考官在面試的整個過程中都感受到你對公司的熱忱。

由於台灣兩大航空公司常會互相出比較題，例如：公益活動等，所以在此章節特別費心整理出台灣兩大航空公司的資訊，請大家特別留意。這樣在面試時不光是在介紹航空公司能用到，碰上比較題或其它難題也不用擔心。

若你在面試時可以說出自己的獨特簡介，而不是一般人都知道的新聞稿，主考官會立即感受到你的用心及對公司的熱忱。當主考官聽了千篇一律的標準答案，你的回答一定能令主考官印象深刻。

以下單元的資訊，尤其針對航點數量，會隨航空公司政策調整，在使用前請再次參考各航空公司官方網站。

大家加油囉！

航空聯盟與航空公司簡介
❷ 航空公司介紹

中華航空（China Airlines）

官方網站：www.china-airlines.com
創始時間：1959 年 12 月 16 日
航　　點：118 個航點
飛機數量：波音、空中巴士等各型航機共 90 架，客機 69 架/貨機
　　　　　21 架
會員制度：華夏會員，天合聯盟
航空旅遊：華航精緻旅遊

注目點

　　親子臥舖（Family Couch）加購——出發日自 2014 年 12 月 1 日起台北往返洛杉磯航線開始，陸續在 2015 年又增設台北往返紐約航線、台北往返舊金山航線、台北往返法蘭克福航線，凡是以 77W 機型飛航之航班均提供 10 組親子臥舖。

　　空服企業培訓服務網－由現職空服人員（包括：空服教師、座艙長等）擔任講師，傳授國際禮儀、接待禮儀等課程，也可針對企業個別所需，量身訂做服務課程。

　　幸福曙光班機：2015 年首度推出「2015 幸福曙光班機」2016 年持續，限量 158 個機位。

公益活動

華航以身為企業公民為責，以自有資源與社會其它專業機構合作從事公益活動。

六大關懷主軸

1. 體育推手：

- **運動賽事贊助** – 2014 年富邦 LPGA 台灣錦標賽、高雄海碩國際男子網球賽、NIKE WE RUN TPE 女性路跑、舊金山灣區華人運動會培育棒球幼苗－資助桃源國小，幫助鼓勵原住民小朋友快樂打球。

- **林書豪籃球公益營** – 2014 年邀請美國職籃 NBA 明星後衛林書豪 Jeremy Lin 擔任特別教練，帶領 30 位小朋友進行趣味籃球體驗。

- **謝淑薇網球營** – 2014 年邀請台灣網球好手謝淑薇擔任特別教練，帶領 30 位小朋友進行訓練。

- **舞動華航路跑活動** – 2014 年舉辦路跑活動，近五千人熱情參與。

2. 教育扎根：

- **航空體驗營** – 號召前後艙組員與國小學童進行航空與英語互動式教學，並捐贈客艙座椅給國內學校，建置飛航情境教室，讓國內飛航教育的幼苗能逐漸茁壯。

- **飛航教育扎根** – 國內獨創以夢想起飛為主軸的體驗營，為讓每個擁有飛航夢想者能夠真實體驗，華航舉辦「青年空服體驗營」、「我愛寶貝體驗營」、「我愛媽咪體驗營」，滿足每顆想飛的心，讓夢想起飛。

- **兒童空服體驗營** – 2014 年為大園鄉國小學童舉辦「兒童空服體驗營」，從美姿美儀開始訓練，再學習迎賓帶位、發送報章雜誌及枕頭毛毯等服務，男學員穿上空服員背心和領帶，女學員換上兒童版改良

式旗袍，實際演練客艙內服務旅客與送餐。

- **志工授課** – 以扶助社會弱勢團體及創造員工心靈滿足為宗旨，招募員工自動自發參與各類不定期公益活動。

- **飛航與英語教學** – 藉由英語教學，定期與大園鄉在地國小學童分享航空知識。

- **愛心趴趴走** – 藉由同仁們的現身說法，透過搭機安全、介紹、餐點、闖關等活動，擴展偏遠地區小朋友的視野。

- **機艙物資捐贈** – 持續捐贈機艙設備，包括：客艙座椅、餐車、餐具、救生設備及電腦硬體……等，讓國內飛航教育能茁壯。

- **創意廚藝競賽** – 2013 年舉辦第一屆華航盃創意廚藝競賽。

- **華航園區參訪** – 包括模擬機教室、機師訓練部門、空服員訓練艙、博物館、修護廠區、調酒教室、美姿美儀教室、逃生訓練與游泳池，由華航專員帶領，並做講解、示範及體驗活動，向外界展現華航空服員的嚴謹訓練制度。

3. **愛心救援：馬來西亞洪災、越南排華暴動、高雄氣爆、日本賑災。**

4. **觀光推廣：**

- **美國花車遊行** – 自 1987 年開始參加美國玫瑰花車遊行，展現台灣特色，連年獲得國際首獎肯定。

- **幸福曙光班機** – 首創國內業界推出國際航班 2015 幸福曙光班機，帶領旅客在高空迎接全台第一道曙光，也是台灣最高的日出。機上有「說故事」機長，一路介紹台灣景點及海岸之美。

- **生態旅遊新航線** – 2013 年首航桃園—山東威海航線，威海市曾榮獲聯合國「改善人類居住環境全球最佳範例城市獎」，最適合生態旅遊的地方。

- **推展文化外交** – 除多次與朱宗慶打擊樂團等具代表性之藝文團體或藝術家合作，2014 年負責運送故宮國寶文物至日本東京與福岡展出，此為重要國寶第一次跨國展出。
- **在地觀光國際化** – 配合政府各項觀光計畫，以實際行動利用航空公司資源，推動及行銷台灣觀光。
- **文創彩繪機** – 結合台灣文創能力，推出彩繪機四部曲－擁抱機、台灣觀光機、台灣部落行旅機、雲門機，讓全球旅客一同感受台灣豐富的文化內涵。

5. 關懷弱勢

- **百圓深耕計畫** – 分為「及人之幼」與「閱讀致富」兩個子計畫，目的在資助育幼院童課後輔導，及提升偏遠地區學童閱讀能力和鼓勵持續閱讀。
- **資深機師協助盲生開飛機** – 華航邀請愛上拍攝飛機的全盲生與全班 30 多位同學，包括班上另外 3 位視障生至桃園總部參觀。4 位盲生進入模擬機艙，讓盲生體驗不同的飛行經驗。
- **鞋盒傳愛** – 在 2013 年，華航透過基督教救助協會所舉辦的「鞋盒傳愛」活動，由同仁們一起響應捐贈文具、生活用品與教育類玩具等物資，讓國內弱勢家庭學童也能度過歡樂的聖誕節。
- **敦親敬老** – 2014 年元月首次舉辦敦親睦鄰歲末敬老活動，前往大園鄉兩所養老院探視，並準備年菜禮盒與年節禮盒。
- **協助癱瘓天使** – 持續與周大觀文教基金會、中華民國喜願協會……等公益團體合作，亦協助國際志工團、義診團物資運送等。
- **慈善義賣** – 金額捐給瑪利亞文教基金會及兒童福利聯盟等弱勢團體。

- **暖暖圍爐** – 秉持回饋鄉里、敦親睦鄰信念,在 2012 和 2013 年與桃園區漁會一同舉辦「歲末圍爐活動」,照顧當地社區弱勢兒童及年長漁民,一同圍爐迎接新年。

6. 愛護地球

- **環境保護** – 鼓勵同仁參與淨灘、淨山與植樹等活動,並積極支持地球日活動,推廣節能觀念。

- **環境治理** – 對環境友善的永續發展企業,結合「文創、科技、環保、信賴、感動」的企業內涵,與環境相協調、對地球永善。

- **環保作為** – **綠能飛航** – 於往返世界各城市的每次飛行,留下更少的碳足跡,用心計較耗油降低量、二氧化碳排放量等各種數據。

- **環境教育** – **環保教育展** – 與環保署、慈濟及素人藝術家聯合設展,為宣傳環保教育、資源回收再利用。

- **電影欣賞** – 舉辦 「+/-2C 電影欣賞與導讀」,讓同仁了解氣候變遷的影響。

- **全員環保活動網頁** – 規劃專屬全員環保活動網頁,使同仁可隨時上網學習。

- **環保活動** – 鼓勵華航人與眷屬,一同參與社會環保活動。

- **知識教育** – 華航進行環保教育訓練,使華航人員具備充足的環保知識。

- **有獎激勵** – 上網填答,有獎激勵華航人了解環保活動推動。

- **環保公益** – 參與國際環保研究計畫,包括全球首架跨太平洋氣候觀測機正式啟航、碳揭露計畫、航空貨運碳足跡工作。在國內參與萬人植樹活動、淨灘活動。

長榮航空（EVA Air）

官方網站：**www.evaair.com**
創始時間：**1989** 年 **3** 月 **8** 日
航　　點：**64** 個航點
飛機數量：**68** 架營運機隊
會員制度：無限萬哩遊、星空聯盟
航空旅遊：長榮假期

注目點

夢幻 Hello Kitty 彩繪機—長榮航空第二代 7 架 Hello Kitty 彩繪機，每架都有獨特的主題故事，包括星空機、牽手機、魔法機、蘋果機、環球機、歡樂機與雲彩機。機上超過 100 項以 Hello Kitty 為主題的服務用品，空服員制服也增添 Hello Kitty 元素，有特製的粉紅色圍裙、徽章等。同時不定期推出各式 Hello Kitty 限量免稅商品。機上依季節烹飪各式 Hello Kitty 風味料理，還特別推出 Hello Kitty 彩繪機專屬網站 evakitty.evaair.com，可上網查詢彩繪機相關動態與最新旅遊產品資訊，同時提供 Hello Kitty 彩繪機桌布下載。

企業社會責任

環境與能源管理

- **溫室氣體盤查 –** 長榮航空支持國際航空運輸協會（IATA）所擬定的減碳策略及目標，自 2011 年起持續針對各種節油減碳、航機減重措施，進行作業程序優化，也持續引進現代化機隊，提升航機燃油使用效率，進而降低溫室氣體排放。

- **噪音防制** – 配合國際民航組織（ICAO）及美國聯邦航空法規（FAR）對航空器出廠時噪音值規範及驗證標準，取得第四級規範，同時遵守各地機場的噪音管制規定及程序，降低機場附近社區因飛機起降產生的噪音衝擊，維護當地社區良好居住品質。

節能減碳

- **飛行計畫最佳化** – 2012 年更換計算更為精準的飛行計畫系統，根據最佳化航路與空層，算出最經濟的載油量，減輕航機起飛重量、降低油耗及溫室氣體排放。
- **飛航操作程序調整** – 若空中交通擁擠無法依計劃高度飛行時，在航管許可情況下，鼓勵飛行員於飛行過程中主動積極要求最佳航機飛行高度，以發揮航機最佳的性能表現，或請求縮短航機飛行距離。
- **航機飛航路線優化** – 定期檢視最佳公告航路資訊，選擇最佳的飛行路線，提高飛行效率。
- **選取較近的備降機場** – 選擇較近的機場作為備降用，減少燃油裝載及碳排放，並定期檢討執行績效。
- **飛機重量及重心控制作業** – 精確計算飛機重量和所需裝載油量，建立完善旅客劃位及行李貨物裝載程序，提供最理想的航機重心位置，提升燃油使用效率，減少二氧化碳排放。
- **機隊現代化** – 自 2003 年開始實施機隊現代化計劃，目前最新型波音 777－300ER 長程環保節能客機成為長程航線的主力機隊，期間也陸續汰換燃油效率相對較低的機型。

慈善公益

　　贊助張榮發基金會－提供物資、機票及人力協助行善，幫助弱勢家庭、偏鄉教育、急難救助與賑災等。

　　捐贈二手愛心資源－將更換過的商務艙餐具捐贈給全台餐飲學校及扶助家庭，捐贈單位包括台灣世界展望會－台東中心、台灣安心家庭關懷協會、聖母醫院及台東基督教醫院等數十個公益團體。

推廣教育

　　長期投入教育公益活動，特別在航空教育方面。除了成立安全教育中心，落實長榮航空的安全教育理念外，並積極投入產學合作，與成功大學和中國民航大學合作，培育航空專業人才，並舉辦國際研討會，與國際接軌。同時贊助聯合報「國際小學堂」專欄，以青少年能了解的方式解讀國際新聞，開拓國內青少年全球視野。

❶ 應試前準備

❷ 應試技巧

❸ 飛上青空情境大模擬

地方回饋

2013 年拍攝「I SEE YOU」廣告後，不但重新詮釋旅遊定義，同時成功推廣台東池上觀光。2014 年為了呼籲旅人珍惜台東觀光資源，更在台東推出一系列活動回饋地方，為台東創造超過 5 億新台幣觀光產值。

為了有效降低因廣告竄紅的池上伯朗大道、奉茶樹等地成為旅遊熱門景點後對當地的衝擊，長榮航空積極協助改善社區秩序，如推出池上環鄉觀光巴士以減少私人車輛進出，讓當地有更好的旅遊品質、定期於金城武廣告的茄冬樹下奉茶，招待往來遊客，傳遞台灣獨有的人情味。

並與台東縣政府及台灣好基金會於池上稻米原鄉館舉辦「長榮航空 I SEE YOU 台東池上奉茶樹裝置藝術發表會」，藉由地標及裝置藝術設置，傳達台東鄉土風情文化。展現高度企業社會責任，也喚醒旅人自發性的自律行為，投射對在地生活及環境的尊重與愛護。

此外，也贊助台東指標性活動之一，「2014 池上秋收稻穗藝術節」，並邀請海外媒體前來採訪，共同宣傳台東池上之美、於 2014 年請日本天皇御用樹醫-山下得男先生及其團隊免費義診「奉茶樹」，守護住民眾的期待、贊助「2014 台灣熱氣球嘉年華」的所有造型熱氣球來台及出國參與活動之貨運載運，以及國際飛行員來台及國內飛行員出國參與活動機票、參與 2014 高雄燈會藝術節、愛、幸福大遊行，吸引國內外旅客來高雄觀光旅遊，帶動當地觀光產業發展。

藝文活動

支持音樂藝文活動，在 2014 年贊助了 Mark Morris 舞團、聖彼得芭蕾舞團、日本飛行劇團、久石讓與維也納國家歌劇院合唱團、馬友友與絲路合奏團等團體。

支持藝文特展－在 2014 年支持國際知名藝文特展來台展覽，唯美‧

巴黎－羅蘭珊畫展、LIFE：看見生活－經典人生攝影展、德古拉傳奇-吸血鬼歷史與藝術特展、Le Petit Prince 小王子特展等。

　　贊助無界限講堂－為鼓勵新加坡之文學、設計、美學、音樂等不同領域之文化藝文交流，於新加坡舉辦無界限講堂，邀請台灣知名導演齊柏林、魏德聖親赴新加坡演講。

　　贊助第 51 屆金馬獎頒獎典禮－鼓勵電影藝術創作者，提升台灣電影文化事業。

體育賽事

　　關注台灣體育發展－贊助國內網球及高爾夫球職業選手，在 2014 年期間，支持國內網球選手-詹詠然與詹皓晴兩姊妹、莊佳容、徐靜雯及高爾夫球選手曾雅妮。在國際級運動賽事贊助，包括 2014 裙襬搖搖 LPGA Classic 美國舊金山女子高球賽、裙襬搖搖 2014 業餘隊際爭霸賽、海碩國際女子網球公開賽與富邦 LPGA 台灣錦標賽等。

　　贊助 2014 璟都慈善盃女子高爾夫球賽-贊助 2014「仁川亞運、盡在華視」轉播活動，讓台灣民眾透過即時轉播一起為中華隊加油。

華信航空（Mandarin Airlines）

官方網站：www.mandarin-airlines.com
創始時間：1991 年 6 月 1 日
航　　點：32 個航點
飛機數量：8 架營運機隊
會員制度：華夏會員
航空旅遊：華信假期

注目點

企業標誌－金色航首的海東青。海東青為黑龍江下游的一種猛禽，期許鷹揚萬里、一飛千里。

以台中為營運基地，是唯一在台中設置專業維修廠的航空公司。2015 年 2 月華信倉儲正式啟用後，提供客、貨運、物流全方位服務，為中台灣創造航空物流環境。

社會公益－愛與關懷－華信航空，送愛到花蓮－透過機票網路競標所得，捐贈花蓮學校，協助學童完成夢想。

飛航做保育－與台北市動物園合作啟動栗喉蜂虎孵育計劃，協助將栗喉蜂虎的棄蛋從金門送至台北。

國泰航空（Cathay Pacific）

官方網站：www.cathaypacific.com

創始時間：1946 年 9 月 24 日

航　　點：近 200 個航點（資訊來源：2015 年 9 月 29 號國泰航空官網新聞稿）**備註：馬德里航線於 2016 年 6 月 2 日啟航。

飛機數量：200 架營運機隊（資訊來源：2015 年 9 月 29 號國泰航空官網新聞稿）

會員制度：亞洲萬里通、馬可孛羅會（Marco Polo Club）

航空旅遊：國泰假期

注目點

國泰航空宣傳口號－翱翔人生（Life Well Travelled）－「用心感受，你會發現旅途有更多可能。寫意翱翔，在於探索。每個轉角，你都可能遇到新的面孔、地方、味道、聲音或氣息。」

國泰航空公司口號－服務發自內心（Service straight from the heart）公益活動－與聯合國兒童基金會合作「零錢佈施」，以旅客外遊後剩餘的外幣，協助貧窮地區兒童改善生活。

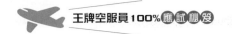
新加坡航空（Singapore Airlines）

官方網站：www.singaporeair.com
創始時間：1947 年 5 月 1 日
航　　點：62 個航點
飛機數量：109 架營運機隊
會員制度：禮遇嘉賓 PPS 俱樂部（The PPS Club）、新航獎勵計
　　　　　劃 KrisFlyer
航空旅遊：新航假期（Singapore Explorer Pass）

注目點

　　新加坡航空宣傳常以新加坡航空空服員為主軸，帶出亞洲優雅、好客與特殊風土人情的企業形象。制服是巴黎服裝大師耶巴曼（Pierre Balmain）設計，採用蠟染印花布料製成的沙龍卡巴雅（Kebaya），四種顏色代表不同級別，成為新加坡航空最具識別的標誌之一。沙龍卡巴雅是新加坡本土華人女性（娘惹）的傳統服飾，上衣是半透明刺繡滾邊，稱為卡巴雅，下半身是沙龍。在空服員招募考試中有一關是試穿制服，可見新加坡航空對空服團隊的宣傳重視。

　　2008 年開始首創在亞洲至美國飛行全商務艙直飛航班（all-Business Class non-stop flights），飛往紐約和洛杉磯。

阿聯酋航空（Emirates Airline）

官方網站：www.emirates.com
創始時間：1985 年 10 月 25 日
航　　點：140 個航點
飛機數量：230 架營運機隊
會員制度：阿聯酋航空 skywards 和 skysurfer

注目點

　　理所當然的尊貴旅程-阿聯酋航空 A380 客機上的頭等艙專屬套房和淋浴水療間、商務艙平躺式座椅、經濟艙寬敞空間和可調式照明、全機艙機上 Wi-Fi 服務，體驗 Google 街景圖首次出現的機艙全貌。頭等艙和商務艙乘客能在機上貴賓休息室與其它乘客盡情互動。

　　阿聯酋航空基金會（The Emirates airline Foundation）-主要在改善孩童生活品質，包括：食衣住行以及教育各方面。例如：斯里蘭卡聖萊昂納孤兒院、衣索比亞 Kindane Mehret 兒童之家。

　　其環境永續經營的承諾──燃油節約、營運節約、生態保育。

①應試前準備

②應試技巧

③飛上青空情境大模擬

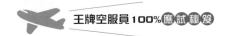
復興航空（TransAsia Airways）

官方網站：www.tna.com.tw
創始時間：1951 年
航　　點：31 個航點
飛機數量：21 架營運機隊
會員制度：龍騰會員
航空旅遊：復興假期

注目點

　　企業實習－與固定學校產學合作，提供大專院校學生實習機會，以培育航空人才。實習內容包括後勤管理、機場服務與航機工程，讓對航空業有夢想的學生能在實習工作中了解航空業，並有機會能成為復興航空正式員工。

　　公益活動－2015 年 11 月，復興航空響應兒童福利聯盟每年 11 月舉辦的「兒童關懷月」活動，全體空服員與地勤人員在工作期間佩戴象徵兒保運動的橘絲帶，為期一個月力挺兒童保護議題。同時在國內機場櫃檯主動發送兒保宣導小卡，每趟飛行旅程也針對嬰幼兒、孩童提供特別服務。

　　橘絲帶運動是在 2005 年，日本小山市發生兩名三、四歲小男孩遭父親及友人虐待致死事件後，當地兒福團體「袋鼠小山」所發起。日本政府從 2007 年起，正式頒定每年 11 月為「兒童虐待防止推進月」，全國一同別上橘色絲帶推動兒童保護運動。台灣兒童福利聯盟從 2013 年開始推行此運動。

立榮航空（UNI AIR）

官方網站：www.uniair.com.tw
創始時間：1996 年
航　　點：26 個航點
飛機數量：16 架營運機隊
會員制度：無限萬哩遊
航空旅遊：立榮假期

注目點

　　立榮金廈一條龍─自 2004 年推出「立榮金廈一條龍」，首創機船聯運一票到底服務，旅客只要一通電話，即可一次訂好機票、船票、金門水頭碼頭與尚義機場間的雙向接駁、行李運送，再透過立榮航空的飛行網路，快速連接金門與台北、台中、嘉義、台南、高雄等五大主要城市，有效節省旅客的時間與體力，成為兩岸小三通的領導品牌及代名詞。

❶ 應試前準備

❷ 應試技巧

❸ 飛上青空情境大模擬

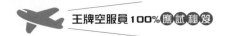
遠東航空（FAT）

官方網站：**www.fat.com**
創始時間：1957 年 6 月 5 日
航　　點：25 個航點
飛機數量：8 架營運機隊
航空旅遊：遠航旅遊

注目點

2015 年與全球最大汽車預訂租賃公司 Rentalcars.com 合作，可在遠東航空官網上預定當地租車，在全球 28000 多個地點為您搜尋最優惠的租車服務。

金廈任我行（小三通服務）—2011 年推出的小三通票券產品，可透過台灣及大陸地區的訂位服務專線，一次訂好機票、船票與地面接送服務。除了金門至廈門外，也提供金門與泉州間最近的選擇。

廉航（廉價航空）

廉航又稱為低成本航空公司（Low cost airlines），指的是將營運成本控制的比一般我們以往熟知的傳統航空公司（Full Service airlines）低的航空公司。廉價航空的機票價格較低，服務項目較一般航空業者精省，所以廉航的空服工作和一般傳統的空服工作有些不同處。

簡單來說，在空中服務時，傳統空服工作送餐點飲料占據許多時間，而廉航的餐點飲料與備品都是旅客額外選購，所以當傳統空服員在送餐點飲料時，廉航空服員就要發揮機上銷售能力銷售這些額外選購項目，當然也包括傳統航空公司的免稅品，所以廉航喜愛的空服員特質和傳統航空公

司也不盡相同。

以威航（V air）在 2015 年 11 月 28 日決選時為例，就談到他們的空服 V 夥伴的特質是臨場反應佳、行事嚴謹，但個性創新活潑。

威航（V air）面試者需經外文口試、團體面試及個人表現等三個階段。團體面試是將面試者分組，針對被指派的題目討論，以最有特色的方式向主考官簡報。題目涵蓋安全（Safety）、服務（Service）與銷售（Sales），測試面試者的團隊合作精神與臨場反應，同時也觀察面試者如何能完成高規格飛安標準，又能提供活力創新服務潛力。

除了台灣廉價航空外，樂桃航空也於 11 月 29 日在台北文華東方酒店舉辦空服人員招募說明會，說明會是以英文與日文為主。所以只要是有飛台灣的航空公司，都會有機會來台灣招募空服員，大家可以隨時留意。

就我個人搭乘經驗，威航空服員在安全示範時，就與傳統航空不同，加入很多可愛動作，真的非常符合他們想要的創新活潑。

威航（V Air）

官方網站：www.flyvair.com
創始時間：2013 年 11 月 15 日
航　　點：6 個航點（曼谷、清邁、名古屋、福岡、大阪、釜山）
飛機數量：5 架營運機隊

注目點

台灣第一家獲准籌備的本土廉價航空，由復興航空全資擁有。初期目標航點為距離台灣 4 小時內的東南亞及東北亞城市，提供全經濟艙服務。

威航英文名稱 V Air 是取 Voyage（旅程）、Vision（願景）、Vivid
（精彩生動）、Victory（勝利）、Venture（探索冒險）之意。企業標誌
（CIS）以台灣黑熊為主體，因為台灣黑熊是「台灣最具代表性的野生動
物」，活動力強且充滿好奇心的特性，加上胸前獨有 V 型標記，正符合 V
Air 的品牌精神。

虎航（Tigerair）

官方網站：www.tigerair.com
創始時間：2013 年 12 月
航　　點：9 個航點、10 條航線（新加坡、曼谷、張家界、澳
　　　　　門、高雄、台北、沖繩、東京成田、東京羽田、大阪）
飛機數量：7 架營運機隊

注目點

中華航空公司與新加坡虎航集團（Tigerair）合資成立台灣虎航
（Tigerair Taiwan），以華航對台灣市場的熟悉結合虎航低成本航空的
DNA 所打造。

樂桃航空（Peach Air）

官方網站：www.flypeach.com

創始時間：2011 年 2 月 10 日

航　　點：9 條國際航線、14 條國內航線（大阪、札幌、仙台、東京成田、東京羽田、松山、福岡、長崎、宮崎、鹿兒島、沖繩、石垣、首爾、釜山、香港、台北（桃園）、高雄 ）**備註：東京（羽田）－首爾（仁川）航線將於 2016 年 2 月 6 日開航東京（成田）－沖繩（那霸）航線將於 2016 年 2 月 20 日開航

飛機數量：14 架營運機隊

注目點

　　樂桃航空的主要股東為全日空（ANA）、第一東方航空及株式會社產業革新機構，公司願景是希望能以日本品牌的低成本航空，成為亞洲地區與日本間的橋樑。

　　樂桃航空是日本首家以關西國際機場作為基地的低成本航空，由全日空 ANA 獨立出資，自主創新經營模式。

香草航空（Vanilla Air）

官方網站：www. vanilla-air.com

創始時間：2011 年 8 月 31 日（日本亞洲航空成立）；2013 年
11 月 1 日更名為香草航空。

航　　點：7 個航點（東京、沖繩、札幌、奄美、香港、台北、高
雄）

飛機數量：8 架營運機隊

注目點

香草航空目前已成為全日空（ANA）獨資。希望能成為如清新的香草
般受人喜愛的新型態低成本航空。

酷航（Scoot Air）

官方網站：www. flyscoot.com

創始時間：2011 年 11 月 1 日

航　　點：26 個航點（新加坡、雪梨、黃金海岸、伯斯、墨爾
本、曼谷、清邁、合艾、喀比、普吉島、天津、西安、
海口、深圳、寧波、廣州、青島、瀋陽、杭州、南京、
香港、台北、高雄、東京、大阪、首爾）

飛機數量：10 架營運機隊

注目點

新加坡的低成本航空，2011 年 5 月由新加坡航空宣告成立。專為年
輕族群、想法年輕的族群和精打細算的族群所創立。選擇酷航就是為了探
索、體驗和享受。

Scootitude（酷航精神）–Reliable（可靠）、Honest（誠實）、Efficient（有效率）、Daring（勇敢）、Friendly（友善）、Refreshing（耳目一新）、Cheeky（幽默）、Smart（聰明 ）、Fun（有趣）、Cool（冷靜）、Safe（安全）、Quirky（多變）、Easy-going（隨和）、Different（與眾不同）、Consistent（一致）、Memorable（難忘的）。

memo

準備報考、邁入航空界

❶ 前言

　　多數航空公司會依據航線擴展策略，在需要招考時在自家網站或新聞媒體公布。也有一些部落客或空服補習班會為應試者收集完整資訊。Facebook 上也有粉絲專頁，例如：空姐瘋，考生能在此獲得最新的應試資訊。

　　為了不錯過任何應試機會，尤其是你心儀的公司，也可加入該公司的 Facebook 並隨時注意該公司網站，這樣也能隨時了解該公司消息，在應試時取得絕對優勢。

選擇即將進入的航空公司

1.航空公司規模、薪資與福利結構

　　應試不單是公司選擇你，同時也是你選擇將要投身的公司。所以在航空公司規模、薪資與福利結構上也是你可以考量的要點。

　　現在網路資訊非常發達，可先在網路上蒐集資料。但建議多花些時間多方參考，不要只看了一個網站或部落格就相信所有資訊，畢竟網路世界是誰都能發表，還是要靠自己歸納所有資訊，判斷這些資訊的可信度。

2.空服員居住地點

　　對我而言，在當空服員前從未去過其它國家，無法想像要在其它國家

生活，所以當時報考的航空公司以能在台灣居住的為主。但我的友人嚮往在異地生活，所以她選擇了國外航空公司。

在這一點上面，請自行考慮自己的性格與家人的意見。雖然還是能常回來台灣，但畢竟在異地生活時間相對很長，所有的生活打理與文化差異都必須自己處理，例如：杜拜航空的華籍空服員就必須在杜拜接受航班派遣，若真要選擇，建議先深入了解派遣地的自然環境、文化習俗等等，評估自己是否能勝任。

同時，報考國外航空公司還有一個大家可能沒想到的地方，就是飛航地點會受限於我們母語。若我們報考其它航空公司，那麼你就是華籍空服員，以需要使用華語的航線為主。當然現在中國遊客大增，連瑞士的錶店都有華語銷售員，所以國外航空公司華籍空服員能飛的航線會大幅增加。但在報考前，還是詳細了解為佳。如果想得到最正確的答案，也可直接向航空公司詢問，不用覺得尷尬。說不定航空公司還會覺得你非常有心加入他們公司，而有意想不到的效益呢？

每家航空公司的要求不同，報名方式也各異，所以須提前了解你想報考航空公司的需求，盡早準備，機會永遠是給準備好的人。

國內外航空招考標準

由於目前約有 240 家航空公司，在此無法詳述每家航空公司對空服員招募的不同需求。但為大家整理分類為以下兩大類：

國內航空公司

包括中華航空、長榮航空、華信航空、復興航空、虎航、威航等。

報考資格

1. 國籍要求：中華民國國籍。
2. 學歷要求：限中華民國教育部認可之國內外大專院校以上畢業，不限科系。持國外畢業證書者，需經由駐外機構認證。
3. 視力要求：矯正後視力達 0.8。
4. 體格標準：符合公司規定（此項規定多半是針對身高，以前航空公司會以身高為標準，但應勞基法規定後，目前多以只要能關上飛機上的艙頂行李箱（約 200-208 公分就算合格）。
5. 英語檢定：通常國內航空公司會要求英語檢定成績，無論是全民英語能力分級檢定測驗、TOEIC、IELTS、TOEFL IBT、TOEFL ITP 或 BULATS。每家航空公司要求的成績標準不同，以下以近期 2015 年 5 月 28 日長榮招募空服員的英語要求標準為例（只需選擇任一項英語檢定並達到標準）：
全民英語能力分級檢定測驗達中級（含）以上程度
TOEIC 達 500 分以上
IELTS 4.0 以上
TOEFL IBT 達 45 分以上
TOEFL ITP 達 450 分以上

BULATS 達 **40** 分以上

6. 報考方式：目前各航空公司多以網路報名，例如中華航空是在自己官方網站報名，復興、遠東航空則是先投遞 **104** 履歷。為避免在報名截止前網路壅塞情況，建議提早完成報名。

應試流程

　　網路報名成功，經航空公司審核合格者，航空公司會以電子郵件方式通知考試時間與地點，所以請確保自己報名填寫的電子郵件信箱地址正確，且一定可以收到電子郵件，謹慎與細心也是空服員必備的基本要素。

1. 面試及筆試：

面試：經過資格審查、儀態評選、服務適職性、中英文面試。

筆試：各家航空公司不一，通常會是英文筆試、心算測驗與適職測驗等等。

備註 可能有讀者好奇，為什麼要心算測驗？因為免稅品販賣也是空服員很重要的工作之一，如果對數字不敏感，販賣免稅品盤點金額短少，可是要空服員自己賠償的喔！

2. 體檢

體檢：航空公司會指定體檢地點，體檢項目為基本的檢查，例如：血液檢驗、心電圖、尿液檢驗等等。

國外航空公司

國外航空公司，其派遣地不在台灣，分佈於世界各地。因應說華語的搭機人數遽增，多數航空公司均有招募華籍空服員的需求。

報考資格

國外航空公司在國籍與學歷要求部分並未像國內航空公司嚴格，通常只要高中畢業資格即可，但在英文方面卻是十分要求。不僅要會話流利，讀寫能力也要在水準以上。

英語檢定成績

多數國外航空公司不會事先要求需具備何種英語檢定成績，多是在面試時直接評量應試者的英文程度。面試除了有主考官與應試者的交談，還會有小組討論，在小組討論時，主考官除了了解應試者的英語能力，同時也在評量應試者的人格特質，請一定要踴躍發言，積極參與討論。

體格標準

國外航空公司對於體格的要求較高，尤其在身型部分，所以體態的健康勻稱非常重要。

在身高部分亦無嚴格限制。但對於能否順利在飛機上工作的評量，和國內航空公司類似，是看應試者手臂日後能否在工作中自由伸展。

以卡達航空（Qatar Airways）為例，要求應試者的手臂需能碰觸212 公分高處（摸高測試）。

人格特質

　　國外航空公司非常注重人格特質,通常會在招募廣告中提及。樂觀外向、能很快融入異文化是國外航空公司喜歡的人格特質。

準備報考、邁入航空界

❷ 如何得知航空公司招募時間、招募廣告怎麼看與注意重點-以卡達航空為例

　　航空公司會依據公司機隊增加來招募新空服團隊。通常國內航空公司會在自己的派遣中心進行面試，而國外航空公司會選擇五星級飯店進行招募。在招募廣告中，請詳細閱讀每個字句，即使你覺得是不重要的公司敘述，例如：「我們是最具活力與文化的團隊！」，乍看下像是廣告詞，但其實也可能用在你的面試中。若主考官問你對公司的看法，你就可以這麼說：「我從貴公司的招募廣告，了解到貴公司的團隊是最具活力且重視文化的團隊，並立刻感受到我屬於貴公司團隊的一員，迫不及待的想和團隊人員一同工作。」。

　　當然航空公司對應試者的要求、應試時間地點與應試前或面試當天需要準備的文件、面試當天服裝等，更是需要仔細牢記，反覆檢查，確保沒有任何出錯的因素。

　　在看招募廣告前，我想先分享一下空服員的福利與薪資結構。在招募廣告上，通常不會提到需要簽約問題。每家航空公司的簽約年限不同，一年至五年不定，最常出現的簽約年限是三年。因為空服員從進入公司至正式上線，航空公司需要進行許多培訓；而關於薪資的細節如下：

- 空服員薪資結構通常是底薪＋飛航加給＋外站津貼（零用金）

- 底薪：就是每個月的固定薪水。

- **飛航加給**：每家航空公司有基本飛行時數，通常為 50-72 個小時，你的飛航加給會根據你的飛航時數計算，若你當月超過公司規定的飛行時數，超過時數的部分飛航加給也會跟著有不同的計算方式。

- **外站津貼（零用金）**：通常指飛機離地後至飛機重返機場間的外站津貼，每家航空公司的外站津貼不同。

備註 若你所工作的航空公司派遣地不在台灣，那住宿及交通等項目通常會由公司負擔，但也不一定一直是如此，所以在應考前還是要特別注意以下各項關於工作福利的細節：

- **空服員福利**：這裡就不贅述成為空服員可以免費環遊世界之類的，我想這些你已經知道了。

- **優待機票**：在你工作滿一定年限後，你和你的直系親屬就能有免費機票或優待機票。每家航空公司的規定不一，在這不詳加介紹，因為航空公司可能有修訂的可能，為確保資訊的正確性，請大家在面試前特別留意。

- **外站住宿交通與津貼（零用金）**：外站住宿交通是指：當你從派遣地飛航至其它城市，從交通（機場至飯店）與住宿都由航空公司負擔。

備註 在我擔任空服員時，公司所選擇的外站住宿我都覺得很棒。當時我

們在紐約的住宿飯店是在曼哈頓最南端的砲台公園（Battery Park）旁，打開窗就能看到自由女神像，當時真的覺得很幸福。在紐約這個高房價的城市裡，你可以免費住在曼哈頓區精華地點，也不用擔心回程機票費，真的覺得自己是個很幸運的人。

- **外站津貼（零用金）**：航空公司不只負擔你的住宿交通（機場至飯店），你待在國外的每秒鐘都有額外的零用金。所以當你在紐約逛大都會博物館時，公司還會給你零用金，很棒吧！如果你想多賺點錢，就多待在外站，依據薪資結構算法，你的津貼就會增加。

所以當有人問我你們空服員一個月賺多少錢？我都會回答因人因地而異，我沒辦法告訴你正確金額，因為空服員的薪資是浮動的，不是固定的。下面跟大家分享一些航空公司的招募廣告：

卡達航空招募廣告

QR8290–Cabin Crew Recruitment Event Taipei（Females Only）26th July 2015 / Qutar Airways / Doha
　　卡達航空招募編號 8290：卡達空服員台北招募會（限女性），2015 年 7 月 26 日／達航空／多哈

　　備註：卡達航空是有招募男性空服員的，但這次的招考是「只限女性」。想要加入卡達航空的男生們別失望，準備好自己，機會永遠在。

Organization: Qatar Airways

Job Function: Cabin Crew

Division: Cabin Crew

Employment Type: Full Time—Permanent

City: Middle East/ Qatar/ Doha

Last date of application : 25-Jul-2015

Qutar Airways

Welcome to a world where ambitions fly high.

From experienced pilots to dynamic professionals embarking on new careers, Qatar Airways is searching for talented individuals to join our award-winning team.

We take pride in our people-a dynamic and culturally diverse workforce is essential to why we are one of the finest and fastest growing airlines in the world.

We offer competitive compensation and benefit packages.

About Your Job:
"Be part of a story worth telling!
Join our awarding winning 5 Star Cabin Crew team"

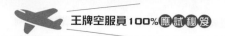

As the National Airline of the State of Qatar, we seek to reflect the best of Qatar's warm and generous hospitality.

Dinner in Paris, Lunch in New York, Breakfast in Montreal, while cruising around the world at 40,000 feet on some of the most modern aircraft in the world is definitely not your typical office job.

Qatar Airways is known to be a truly world class, 5 star global airline, challenging established norms and a leader in airline hospitality.

On the Ground and in the air we offer our customers a powerful approach to service. Our Cabin Crew are Qatar Airways' Ambassadors to the world.

The Qatar Airways Cabin Crew team is growing. We are looking for candidates who can deliver our mission by providing "Excellence in everything we do". Known for our 5 star hospitality, we look for future Cabin Crew who can be part of our " World Class Global Brand:.

Join our multinational Cabin Crew Team and enjoy a tax-free

remuneration package including accommodation, allowances and transportation for duty.

Write your own story with Qatar Airways. World's 5 star airline.

About you:

To be part of this winning team, you need to meet the following requirements :

• Minimum age of 21 years

• Minimum arm reach of 212 cms on tip toes

• Minimum high school education with fluency in written and spoken English

• Willingness to relocate to Doha, Qutar

• Outgoing personality with good–inter personal skills and the ability to work with a multination team.

中文翻譯

公司：卡達航空
職稱：空服員
部門：空服組員
職位類型：全職
城市：中東／卡達／多哈
報名截止日：2015 年 7 月 25 日

卡達航空
歡迎來到飛翔的世界。

我們經驗豐富的機師與充滿活力的專業團隊與你一同開展新的事業。卡達航空在尋找有才能的人加入我們的得獎團隊。

我們擁有令人自豪、最具活力與文化的團隊，這就是我們成為世界發展最好最迅速航空公司之一的因素。

我們提供最具競爭力的優渥條件。

關於你的工作：
加入我們五星級得獎空服團隊，成為值得傳唱故事的一員

我們不斷試著傳達卡達溫暖且大方好客的特質。

在巴黎晚餐、紐約午餐、蒙特利爾早餐，你在 40,000 呎高空乘坐世界最摩登的飛機，在世界各地旅行，這絕非一般典型的辦公室工作。

卡達航空絕對是世界頂尖、五星級的全球航空，挑戰制式的成規，是航空界的典範。

我們提供顧客從地面到高空最好的服務，我們的空服組員是卡達航空的大使。

卡達航空的空服團隊正在成長。我們在尋找能傳達我們的使命「做所有事都要完美」的一員；卡達有五星級的服務，我們正在尋找能成為我們全球品牌的你。

加入我們多國籍空服團隊，享受免稅的薪資福利，包括住宿、外站津貼和交通。

與世界五星級的卡達航空一起寫下屬於你的故事。

關於你：
想成為我們團隊一員，你需要符合下列條件：

- 21 歲以上
- 手指尖需能碰觸 212 公分高處
- 高中以上學歷，英語說寫流利
- 願意移居到卡達的多哈居住
- 個性外向，人際交往技巧佳，有能力與多國籍團隊工作

備註 每家航空公司要求的學歷不同，通常國外航空公司對學歷與英語能力證明文件要求不高，他們真正重視的是你在面試時是否能表現出符合公司需求的特質。

前輩經驗巧巧說

以前航空公司會有身高限制，但現在是以手臂摸高來取代量身高的步驟。通常在面試時，牆上會有一條線請你觸碰，而這條線通常就是飛機座位上方行李置物櫃（overhead bin）的高度；卡達航空在此是把高度直接告知。以前常有人跟我說，為什麼空服員一定要限制身高，難道不高的人就沒有空服員特質嗎？以前還有來量身高的應試者，把包頭綁在頭頂上，希望能通過身高限制，結果馬上被要求把頭髮拆掉。事實上，如果你的身高不夠，是真的沒辦法在飛機上獨立工作的。就算沒有旅客需要你幫忙放行李，有時航班客滿時，你也需要重新安排行李置物位置，因為不是所有旅客都能將行李擺置整齊。最重要的是，機上廚房裡有很多置物櫃的高度可能比行李置物櫃更高，大家都在忙的時候，誰能有空來幫你拿用品？你也不可能每趟航班都請人幫忙吧？所以空服員的身高限制真的不是一種歧視或是不平等條款，而真的是工作需求。

The Event :

Venue: THE WESTIN TAIPEI–133 NO.3, Section 3, Nanjing E Rd, Taipei, Taiwan 104

Date: 26th July 2015

Time: Anytime between 9 am to 5 pm

Attire: Formal Business attire

Bring along:

- 1x CV
- 1x passport photocopy
- 1 x passport photograph taken in the same dress code mentioned above (without glasses).
- 1 x full length photograph taken in the same dress code mentioned above (without glasses).
- 1 x photocopy of your highest education certificate (in its original language is fine).

Note: you will be required to attach the following:

1. Resume/ CV
2. Recent Full Length Color Photo
3. Copy of Highest Education Certificate
4. Copy of Passport

中文翻譯

招募會：

地點：台北威斯汀六福皇宮飯店——台北市南京東路三段 133 號

日期：2015 年 7 月 26 日

時間：上午 9 點至下午 5 點

場地：正式會議廳

請攜帶：

- 一份履歷表
- 一份護照影本
- 一張護照大頭照（不戴眼鏡）
- 一張全身照（不戴眼鏡）
- 一份最高學歷證書影本（無須翻譯成英文）

注意：你將被要求繳交：

1. 履歷表
2. 彩色全身近照
3. 最高學歷證書影本
4. 護照影本

備註 全身照的選擇：這裡有特別強調不戴眼鏡，但除了不戴眼鏡之外，還有什麼地方能為面試加分的？

前輩經驗巧巧說

　　有些航空公司會特別強調不接受沙龍照，我個人也建議就算航空公司沒有特別說明，也不要繳交沙龍照。生活照的重點在於「生活」這兩個字，航空公司請你繳交「生活」照，就是想看看你的生活。那你要如何呈現你的生活呢？我建議看報考公司的文化與要求的空服員特質。這時你覺得無聊的公司簡介和招募廣告就派上用場囉！你除了可以從網路，或你可能參加的空服員補習班給你的建議，決定照片風格。我個人覺得只要從公司簡介和招募廣告中就能找出答案。

　　舉例來說，如果航空公司在網站和招募廣告中強調的是活潑，那你繳交一張在安靜看書的照片可能就不是那麼適合，是吧？其實就是那麼簡單，別想的太複雜，把這個時間用來充實自己的其它能力對應試更有效率。

　　決定好生活照風格後，我的建議就只有三點囉！簡單乾淨的背景、清楚的人像與人見人愛的笑容。

1. **簡單乾淨的背景**：最重要的重點就是裡面除了你之外，不要有第二個人，主考官應該不想玩猜謎遊戲吧？其它該穿什麼衣服？該搭配什麼妝髮等等的，網路上可以找到很多資訊，但我個人覺得，與其勉強自己刻意要穿什麼服裝、搭配什麼妝髮，不如就以自己的風格呈現有自信的自己。當然如果你平日的風格是極端的性感或搖滾之類的，就還是聽聽別人的建議吧！

2. **清楚的人像**：繳交生活照主要是要讓主考官在面試前先見到你，因為畢竟護照上的大頭照限制很多。所以五官清楚是最基本的吧！我個人建議，美肌功能也別過度使用，因為主考官最終還是會見到真實的你，所以真的別過度修飾了，記得這是「生活」照，主考官想看到的就是你平時生活的樣子，自然就好。

3. **人見人愛的笑容**：出自真心的笑容最吸引人，所以別在乎自己有沒有露齒，還是要露幾顆牙齒之類的，除非你像演員或模特兒進行過特別訓練，否則心裡想著要注意這麼多的重點，笑容要怎麼自然呢？我覺得放輕鬆最重要。多拍幾張，一定能找出主考官對你一見鍾情的照片。

❶ 應試前準備

❷ 應試技巧

❸ 飛上青空情境大模擬

準備報考、邁入航空界

❸ 招募廣告怎麼看與注意重點-以全日空航空招募消息為例

全日空航空招募廣告與注意重點

　　以下招募消息與上篇廣告說明標示一樣，重點是說明這一家航空公司與其他家不同的資歷要求（例如多益成績）、是否有特殊要求，或是提出一般航空公司都會要求的相同項目等。先看英文，熟悉全英文的模式，提前作好心理準備！

BENEFITS & REQUIREMENTS:

All Nippon Airways aims to be a leading company for the world in Customer Satisfaction and Value Creation, by generating new value in our service delivery.

On behalf of our client ANA"Japan's 5 star airline", SASS Associates Grp is looking for young and aspiring individuals to be Cabin Attendants with passion.

All Nippon Airways Cabin Attendant Recruitment.

We are looking for Cabin Attendants with a combination of professionalism and sophistication to provide excellent customer satisfaction and value creation.

REQUIREMENT:
- PERMANENT TAIWAN RESIDENT STATUS ONLY
- TOEIC SCORE OF 650 & ABOVE
- JAPANESE LANGUAGE IS ADVANTAGE
- PLEASANT PERSONALITY

- MINIMUM DEGREE QUALIFICATION
- AT LEAST 18 YEARS OF AGE

SERVICE BENEFIT:
- FREE & DISCOUNTED TRAVEL
- MATERNITY& SPECIAL LEAVE
- ANNUAL LEAVE

1 應試前準備

2 應試技巧

3 飛上青空情境大模擬

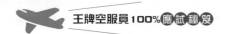
APPLY ONLINE:

1. Personal Data

    Family Name as per Passport

    Gender

    Nationality

    Name (in Local Language Characters) National ID

    Date of Birth

    Age

    Country of Birth

    Place of Birth (City)

    Religion

    Marital Status

    Passport information

    Passport No.

    Passport Country of issue

    Passport Issue Date

    Passport Expire Date

    Contact information

    Email Address

    Please re-enter Email Address

    Home Telephone

    Mobile Phone

    Home Address (English Version)

    Home Address (Local Language Version)

2. Personal Info:

Please attach a passport photo of yourself (10 MB File Size Restriction. Best recommended Size (400X500 pixies).

Weight :

Height :

Date of Commencement if Selected:

3. Education

Please list your highest qualification first

From

To

School/ Institution

Country

Qualification

4. Language Proficiency

Please list your language proficiency from very fluent to little

Language

Spoken (Little / Fluent / Very Fluent)

Written

Name of Certification (if any)

Grade Level (if any)

5. Employment History

   From

   To

   Company

   Position

   Salary (as per local currency)

   Reason of Leaving

6. Family Particulars:

   Name of Family Members

   Relationship

   Age

   Occupation

7. Other Info:

   · Have you been ever convicted for a crime in your country ? Yes / No

   · Have you ever had any serious illness or injury?

   · Are you required to have medication on a regular basis?

   · Have you ever been declared bankrupt?

   · Have you ever been interviewed by Sass Associates Grp or All Nippon Airways previously for Cabin Attendant?

   · Do you have any scars that would be visible in uniform?

- Are you have any family member (s) or relatives working in Sass Associates or All Nippon Airways?

In the event of emergency, please contact:

- Name (Emergency Contact Name)
- Contact No.
- Relationship

How do you know about this recruitment campaign?

I agree that Sass Associate Grp ("SASS" may collect, use and disclose the information that I have provided in this form for the purpose of this job application, other employment opportunities, and for providing marketing information that SASS, SASS's affiliates, business partners and related companies may be offering, which I have agree to receive, in accordance with the Personal Data Act 2012 (Singapore).

Please click the relevant box if you agree to receive via: (Email, Text Message, Phone Call)

I declare that the above particulars are true, updated and correct to the best of my knowledge. Any misrepresentation or omission of facts provided is sufficient cause of cancellation for employment or dismissal from the Company's service upon employment.

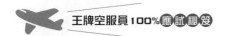
中文翻譯

福利與招募需求：
全日空航空公司的目標是透過我們的服務創造新的價值，並在顧客滿意度與創造價值方面成為世界領先公司。

新加坡人力仲介公司 SASS Associate Grp 代表客戶全日空航空公司，尋找年輕有抱負的新血，帶著熱情加入我們客艙組員行列。

全日空航空公司招募：
我們正在尋找專業又有修養的客艙組員，與我們一起提供卓越的顧客滿意度，創造新的價值。

招募需求：
• 永久台灣籍人士
• TOEIC 成績 650 分以上
• 具日文程度優先考慮
• 令人愉悅的個性
• 符合最基本學歷要求
• 年齡 18 歲以上

福利：
• 免費及折扣旅遊
• 產假及特別假
• 年假

網路申請：

1. 個人資訊

    護照上的姓拼音

    性別

    國籍

    姓名（中文）

    身分證字號

    出生日期

    年齡

    出生國家

    出生地

    宗教

    婚姻狀態

    護照資訊

    護照號碼

    護照簽發國家

    護照簽發日期

    護照過期日

    聯絡資訊

    電子郵件地址

    請重新輸入電子郵件地址

    住家電話

    行動電話

    住家地址（英文）

① 應試前準備

② 應試技巧

③ 飛上青空情境大模擬

住家地址（中文）

2. 個人資訊

請上傳護照上個人照片（**10MB** 以下，建議 **400X500** 畫素，檔案型式 **GIF**、**JPEG**、**PNG**）

體重

身高

開學日期（如果選擇）

3. 教育

請先列出最高學位

從

到

學校

國家

資格

4. 語言能力

請列出語言能力，從非常流利到略懂

語言

說（略懂／流利／非常流利）

寫

認證資格（如果有的話）

認證等級（如果有的話）

5. 工作經歷

   從

   到

   公司

   職位

   薪資（當地貨幣）

   離職原因

6. 家庭狀況

   家庭成員姓名

   關係

   年齡

   職業

7. 其它資訊

   ・ 你在你的國家有犯罪紀錄嗎？ 有／沒有

   ・ 你有任何重大疾病或外傷嗎？

   ・ 你必須定時服用任何藥物嗎？

   ・ 你有宣告破產的記錄嗎？

   ・ 你之前有在 Sass Associates Grp 或全日空航空公司應徵空服員
     的經驗嗎？

   ・ 你有任何傷疤是穿制服會很明顯嗎？

   ・ 你有家人或親戚在 Sass Associates 或全日空航空公司工作嗎？

若有緊急事件，請聯絡：

- 姓名（緊急聯絡人姓名）
- 聯絡電話：
- 關係：

你如何得知這項招募消息？

依據 2012 年個人資料法（新加坡），我同意 Sass Associate Grp 使用並同時願意接受「SASS」可能會收集，使用和披露您對這個工作機會所提供的資訊， 將這些資訊用於 SASS、SASS 子公司、企業夥伴及相關公司的行銷活動。

若您同意接受，請勾選您想經由何種管道接受（電子郵件信箱、簡訊、電話）

我聲明上述資訊是真實的，我會盡我所能地更新以維持資訊正確。若有提供任何虛假陳述或遺漏，願意接受解雇處分。

memo

準備報考、邁入航空界

❹ 資料填寫實例說明

以中華航空公司最近一次招考時程為例：

8/14-8/30 線上履歷登錄

9/12 週末初試

9/19 週末複試

9/20 公佈體檢名單

線上履歷報名：http://calec.china-airlines.com/recruit/recurit_104EZO8/recruit.asp

報名資格：

（一）具有教育部認可學士學位或以上者。

　　1. 國內學歷者，需備妥畢業證書及在校各學期含操行之成績單。

　　2. 國外學歷者，所備之畢業證書及成績單均需經駐外機構認證。

　　3. 大陸學歷者，需備有教育部相當學歷證明、畢業證書及在校各學期成績單。

　　4. 應屆畢業生尚未取得畢業證書者，初試時請攜帶學生證及在校各學期成績單；通過甄試報到時仍未取得畢業證書者，將視同自動放棄，不得有任何異議。

（二）具備以下任何一項英檢成績：（2013/10/1 以後取得之成績）：TOEIC/600 分、BULATS/45、IELTS/4.5 或 TOEFL ITP/480、iBT/64 等以上成績。

備註 TOEIC 曾針對華航招募推出特別考試場次，提供快速出成績單服務。但還是建議提早把測試成績準備好，以免錯失難得的招考機會。

（三）男性需攜帶退伍令、除役、免役或待退等相關證明文件正本，2015/11/2 以後退伍者請勿報名。

（四）改名或繳交英文文件資料者，請攜帶相關佐證證明。

備註 相關佐證證明包括國外學歷證書等，請詳盡詢問航空公司需要何種佐證證明。

報名及工作說明：

（一）工作地點與任務：依本公司安排，以台北為派飛基地。

（二）報名日期：自 2015/8/14 中午 12:00 至 2015/8/30 夜間 23:59。

（三）本公司各階段甄試結果均以線上查詢方式公告，恕不另行通知。

甄試流程說明：

（一）報名資格審核：審核應試人員系統報名資料（網路報名資料一經送出無法修改）。

（二）作業時間：網路報名結束後開始。

（三）初試面試場次公告查詢：2015/9/9 中午 12:00 至 2015/9/11 夜間 23:59。

（四）初試：書面資料審核、面試。

（五）甄試時間：預計於 2015/9/12 舉行。

（六）初試結果公告查詢：預計於 2015/9/13 中午 12:00 至 2015/9/15 夜間 23:59。

（七）複試：面試、服務專業職能評量。

1 應試前準備

2 應試技巧

3 飛上青空情境大模擬

（八）甄試時間：預計於 2015/9/19 舉行。

（九）複試結果公告查詢：預計於 2015/9/20 中午 12:00 至 2015/9/22 夜間 23:59。

　　（1）通過複試之應試人員需於複試結果查詢系統開放時間內選取體檢日期。

　　（2）體檢日期共三梯次，分別為 9/21、9/22、9/23，每梯次員額均有限制，額滿需選擇其它梯次。

　　（3）體檢日期一經登錄，恕無法變更。未登錄選取體檢日期，或登錄後未依時間體檢者，視同自動放棄客艙組員甄試。

　　（4）綜合評量：複試面試成績、體格檢查、職前調查及英文檢定成績。應試人員無須到考。綜合評量結果公告查詢：將於 2015/10/16 中午 12:00 至 2015/10/18 夜間 23:59。

（十）受訓報到：預計 11/09 開始分梯受訓，每梯次均有員額限制，額滿需選擇其它梯次。通過綜合評量之正取人員需於綜合評量查詢系統開放時間內選取報到日期。受訓報到日期一經登錄，恕無法變更。未登錄選取受訓報到日期者，或選取後未依時間報到者，視同自動放棄客艙組員甄試。

登錄表單需填寫下列資料：

- 英文檢定項目
- 考試日
- 分數
- 其它語言能力：台語、日語、韓語、義語
- 中文姓名
- 性別

- 身分證號或居留證號
- 原住民
- 出生日期
- 最高學歷
- 學校
- 科系
- 是否在台灣設有戶籍
- 具護士／護理師專業證照

備註 護士／護理師專業證照對於應試空服員真的是一個非常大的優勢。因為飛機上除了你在新聞上看到的可能有生子外，還有各種不同的醫護問題。如果我是主考官，有護士／護理師專業證照我一定會加很多分，因為這是空服團隊很需要的。

- 服役情形
- 役畢／待退日期
- 婚姻
- 是否有親屬（直系親屬或兄弟姊妹）任職（含曾任）華航

備註 這部分請誠實填寫。就我個人的經驗，有親屬在同公司應該是加分的選項。像我曾任職的航空公司就非常喜歡錄取姊妹檔，我們公司有非常多的姊妹檔。事實上，我妹妹也是晚我一年進入同一間航空公司的。

- 聯絡電話
- 行動電話
- 戶籍地址

- 電子信箱
- **Facebook**

備註 關於 Facebook 部分，我真心覺得不要發表過於激烈的批評言論，無論是政治、宗教或其它議題。上傳的照片也要慎選，別把 Facebook 當成你自己和朋友的相片簿。因為不認識你的人，如果有了你的 Facebook，就會不自覺地從你的 Facebook 中了解你。若你的 Facebook 有特別引人注意的地方，例如：太性感的照片或跟一堆人瞎混胡鬧的照片，建議能先處理掉就處理掉吧！萬一主考官真的看到了你的 Facebook，在面試時問了你關於性感照片的問題，你再怎麼解釋自己也沒用。

- 工作經歷／社團經驗（50 字內）
- 中文自傳（500 字以內，超過字數限制您將無法報名）
- 英文自傳（1000 字元內，超過字數限制您將無法報名）

備註 以上工作經歷／社團經驗、中文自傳與英文自傳撰寫，請參考第 100-101 頁與第 126～135 頁的頁說明。若是你還有時間能累積工作經驗或社團經驗的話，能接觸最多人、與人溝通協調的經驗是最值得累積的。

前輩經驗巧巧說

　　工作：服務業、餐飲業、飯店業或其它產業的公關或客服部門都是很值得考慮的。因為能直接面對顧客，磨練應對技巧，訓練應變能力。若是能用得上英文或是其它的外語能力，更能增加自己在應試時的競爭力。

　　社團：我覺得與其選擇社團，不如選擇社團中的位置，例如：社團公

關、社長。因為如果你本身不是很愛孩子，硬要你為了空服員的這份工作加入康輔社，那你在不開心的情況下，也沒辦法真正體會到什麼能跟主考官分享的吧!所以就選一個你喜愛的社團，然後爭取社長或公關的位置吧！

　　報考方式：國外航空公司通常會在五星級大飯店內舉辦招募，時間為上午 9 點至下午 5 點。應試者先在航空公司網站回覆招募訊息，當日至指定地點應試。

　　應試流程：初試（Open Day）：只要有興趣的人都可以直接去應試，所以請提早至考場。因為通常人都非常多，若你太晚去，有可能連交履歷的機會都沒有。

　　請應試者務必將招募公司規定的文件帶齊。英文履歷、大頭照、全身彩色近照、最高學歷證書影本、護照影本是多數國外航空公司的基本要求。

　　通過初試（Open Day），即可進入複試（Assessment Day）：複試（Assessment Day）：通常為抽題後進行小組討論，例如城市介紹，討論後輪流發表。

　　筆試：各家航空公司不一，通常為文法、單字、閱讀等，有時可能還會考英文寫作。

　　最終面試（Final Interview）：主考官會以英文發問，問題多半圍繞在工作經驗、團隊合作、情緒處理、在異地生活等等。

　　國外航空公司視招募人數而定，通常為今日初試，隔日複試。所以幾乎初試結束馬上知道應試結果。

chapter 3

自薦信、履歷、自傳撰寫

❶ 前言

　　航空公司招考時，會先透過照片和文字初步了解你。所以除了照片外，文字部分通常會要求應試者繳交自薦信（Cover Letter）、履歷表（Resume）與自傳（Autobiography）。由於網路的發達，越來越多的航空公司採取線上報名方式，在文字資料的準備會相對來說越來越容易。但目前還是有些航空公司要求這三項完整的文字資料，所以在這單元將和大家一起準備專屬於你的文字介紹。請大家不要只把它當作必須繳交的資料而已，主考官很有可能會在你準備的這些資料中，找出面試你的問題。所以還是那句話，無論你找到再多別人的範例，都只能當作你的參考，請勿照本宣科，而要認真思考關於你自己的人生，讓主考官在你準備的文字資料當中，就能看出你是個有獨立思考和判斷能力的最佳空服員人選，這才是真正的價值所在。先跟大家分享一下這三項文字資料的意義：

● 自薦信（Cover Letter）

　　以我們目前常使用的電子郵件來舉例，自薦信就是你要傳一個帶有附件（履歷和自傳）的電子郵件給陌生人時所寫的內文。簡單明瞭吧？沒字面上看起來那麼嚴肅複雜。

　　因為是陌生人，所以重點就是要讓陌生人知道你是誰？為什麼要傳這封郵件？附件是什麼？如果收件者對收到的電子郵件有疑問時，可以怎麼跟你聯絡？

◉履歷（Resume）

　　履歷就是你無法作假和過度美化的過去人生，所以也不用想太多，如果是線上報名，要你填什麼就填什麼，只有一個重點，誠實作答。因為你寫在履歷上的過去都是很容易查詢的，例如：你的學校科系、你曾待過的公司等等。就算你覺得不滿意你的過去經歷，但那已成事實。況且就算你覺得不滿意，只要你和我一起跟著這本書建立正確心態，願意相信所有的事都有一體兩面，你不滿意的地方也有它可取之處，所以千萬不要抱持著僥倖心理，因為擔心而作假，這樣絕對沒有勝算，拜託大家相信我囉！

◉自傳（Autobiography）

　　自傳和履歷都在讓主考官了解你，但切入點不同，自傳不像履歷，是可以美化的，你可以寫些內在的自己，履歷上看不到的你。但就是因為可以美化，所以需要花些精神。

　　一般來說，自傳就是文字的自我介紹，但除了你的姓名可以重複外，請不要浪費字數（通常航空公司會限制自傳字數），寫履歷上就有的資訊。例如：年齡、家庭狀況、星座之類的，除非這些訊息有特別的故事。

　　但對我而言，自傳不單只是文字的自我介紹，我想達到：「看自傳的陌生人對我產生好奇心和好感，想進一步認識我。」的目標。好奇心是人類的天性，只要有好奇心，就會想要尋找答案。試想對你自傳有好奇心的主考官要怎麼尋找答案呢？當然就是從你的身上才能找到答案。當其他應試者在自傳中寫「我的家庭美滿」、「有兩個兄弟姊妹之類的」，你覺得誰比較有面試勝算？這時你可能在想，我要怎麼引起主考官的好奇心，讓他想進一步了解我呢？其實答案很簡單，對不認識你的人來說，什麼資訊都能引起他的好奇心。當然你提供的資訊要跟你想從事的空服工作有關。

自薦信、履歷、自傳撰寫
❷ 關於自薦信（Cover Letter）

　　雖然現在很多航空公司都採取網路報名方式，不需要自薦信（Cover Letter），但還是有些航空公司會要求應試者繳交自薦信（Cover Letter）；自薦信和自傳的寫法完全不同，自薦信就是信，所以不要超過信的尺寸，簡明扼要是最好的，但簡明扼要才是最難表達的。以下是撰寫自薦信的重點：

1. 三段表述法

　　第一段：為什麼想要應徵這個工作？

　　第二段：為什麼你是這個工作的最佳人選？

　　第三段：感謝結尾。

2. 內容勿與履歷內容重覆

　　寫出自己與這個工作最相關的部分，這個工作非你莫屬的地方。

3. 內容精準具說服力

　　寫目前的狀況，例如學歷就寫最高學歷、工作就寫最近的一份工作，專長就寫與職位最直接相關的專長，開門見山，一目了然。

4. 重點放前面

　　重點放在每個段落的第一句，之後的句子是用來說明與佐證你所描述的重點。

自薦信（Cover Letter）參考寫法：

➢ 聯絡方式（姓名、地址、電話、e-mail 信箱）
➢ 對方稱呼（招聘經理／人力資源經理：Dear Hiring Manager / Human Resource Manager）

➢ 內文：
　第一段：為什麼想要應徵這個工作？
　第二段：你為什麼是這個工作的最佳人選？
　第三段：感謝結尾

➢ 結尾署名 ：
Sincerely 或 Cordially 或 Respectfully,
Lillian Tsai

　　正式的自薦信（Cover Letter）都是要親自簽名的。若是以繳交紙本的形式，當然沒問題。但若公司要求以電子檔的形式傳送，千萬不要怕麻煩，把檔案以紙本的形式印出來，親自簽名後，掃描成電子檔再傳送。對自薦信（Cover Letter）來說，親自簽名的步驟是很重要的。

1 應試前準備

2 應試技巧

3 飛上青空情境大模擬

剛畢業，尚未有過正式工作經驗者。以在校內參與的相關活動為撰寫內容。別擔心，無論什麼樣的校內社團或校外活動，都能與空服員的工作相結合。因為空服員的工作最重要的就是與人接觸和溝通。當然，如果你現在還在校，還有機會參與活動的話，能參與和外國人溝通頻繁的活動當然更能加分，因為這樣的活動能直接顯現你的英語能力。這樣的活動相信校內很多，若從校內找不到或不符合你的需求，像接下來範例中所寫的外國人協助中心或台灣一些大的慈善基金會都有很多這樣的機會可參與。

已經工作想轉職，但覺得自己目前的工作和空服員不相關，不知道該怎麼下筆嗎？記得，還是那句話，空服員的工作最重要的就是與人接觸和溝通。我想無論你做什麼樣的工作，一定都需要與人接觸和溝通，所以無論是什麼工作，都與空服員的工作相關，差別只是在關聯性的強弱。而關聯性的強弱也只是以一般人的思考邏輯判定，若你能在一般人覺得關聯性弱的工作經驗中，寫出關聯性強的部分，那更能吸引應試公司的注意。

例如：你可能現在是個程式設計師，一般人可能認為程式設計師就是每天在座位上埋首於電腦的宅男。但也許你是每天需要跟來自全世界程式設計師聯絡的工程師，或是，你透過這個工作，認識了許多在台灣工作，不同國籍的程式設計師，而且常常有國際聚會。這些也都是很好的實例經驗分享。

　　所以撰寫自薦信（Cover Letter）一點都不難，只要將下列範例中的第一段只需根據你的活動內容小幅修改，第二段活動內容改成你自己從事過的，而第三段只需將你的聯絡方式改成你自己的後，完整的自薦信就完成了。

　　當然在第二段中，還是建議別用漂亮的形容詞包裝自己，這樣可說是浪費版面。雖然只是自薦信（Cover Letter），您可能會這麼想，而且你可能也知道很多航空公司儘管會要求自薦信（Cover Letter），卻不一定會仔細閱讀。不過，既然花時間寫了，就要當作應試公司所要求的一個重要事項，跟你自身有關的實際案例還是需要的。所以像我思想成熟（Mature）、為人誠實（Honest）或能獨立作業（Ability to work independently），這些用漂亮的形容詞堆積出來的句子就不用出現在自薦信（Cover Letter）上了。當然如果你真的想不出什麼實例，又想全心完成符合航空公司要求的一份自薦信，那麼你就更要將心力放在公司要求的自薦信，而不是形容詞的堆疊上了。

自薦信（Cover Letter）參考範例一

撰寫人背景說明

剛畢業，尚未有過正式工作經驗者。

Lillian Tsai　　　　　　　　　　　　　　　　　　　◀ 英文姓名

10F-2,No. 1, Fuzhou St., Zhongzheng Dist.,

Taipei City100, Taiwan(R.O.C.)　　　　　　　　　◀ 英文地址

+886 2 2351- 2007　　　　　　　　　　　　　　　◀ 聯絡電話

XXXX@gmail.com ◀ 電子郵件信箱

October 10, 2015 ◀ 英文日期

Human Resource Manager ◀ 人力資源經理

XXXX Airlines XXXX ◀ 航空公司

11 W 53rd St, New York, NY 10019, United States ◀ 航空公司英文地址

Dear Human Resource Manager,

I learned about the flight attendant position on your website. I completed my Bachelor's Degree with a major in Spanish from Tamkang University in July, 2015. The flight attendant position appeals to me because it requires flexibility, initiative, and the ability to collaborate with a team in order to deliver excellent service to passengers. Throughout my college, I have participated in voluntary and international social activities which have allowed me to develop the skills you required.

During the summer 2014, as a voluntary Chinese teacher of Foreigners Assistance Center, I assisted people from all over the world to study Chinese by making training materials including daily conversation and information about how to live in Taiwan. This is a valuable experience for me to thrive in my future flight attendant career. Meanwhile, I learned how to communicate with foreigners from different countries and had lots of materials to share with my future passengers. I am confident that I have the ability to contribute in this position and your esteemed company.

The prospect of becoming a member of your team would be an exciting challenge. If you have questions, I may be reached at +886 2 2351 2007 or XXX@gmail.com.

Thank you for your time and consideration.

Sincerely,
Lillian Tsai

中文翻譯

人力資源經理您好，

我從貴公司網站上了解貴公司正在招聘空服員。我在 2015 年 7 月從淡江大學西班牙語系畢業，空服員對我而言是需要具備彈性、積極主動與團隊合作的工作，才能將最好的服務帶給旅客。從我在求學生涯參與的志願工作和國際社會活動，讓我能將自己發展成具備貴公司所尋找的空服特質。

在 2014 年夏天，我擔任外國人在台協助中心的中文老師，協助來自

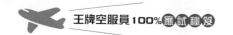

世界各地的外國人學習中文。在這個志願工作中,我自己做了訓練教材,包括中文日常對話與如何在台灣生活。這對我而言是我於未來職涯-空服員蓬勃發展很寶貴的經驗,我也學習到如何跟不同國家的外國人溝通,也累積了許多資訊想與我未來的旅客分享。我有信心能為貴公司在空服員的團隊中貢獻一己之力。

　　能有機會成為您團隊的一員對我而言是個非常欣喜的挑戰,若您有任何疑問,請以電話 +886 2 2351 2007 或電子郵件信箱 XXXX@gmail.com 聯絡我。

　　謝謝您的時間與考慮!

誠摯地

Lillian Tsai

自薦信(Cover Letter)參考範例二

撰寫人背景說明

從外商航空公司轉本土航空公司的應試者。

　　從外商航空公司轉本土航空公司,建議強調自己過往的空服經驗能為公司帶來的貢獻。但因為同樣是空服員工作,所以要轉換回本土航空公司,主考官最好奇的應該就是你的轉職理由。最容易被理解的轉職理由就是家庭因素。

　　與其讓主考官猜測你的轉職理由,不如就在推薦信上直接寫出轉職理

由，直接解決主考官心中疑惑，讓主考官覺得你有直接面對問題，又了解人心的人格特質，這未嘗不是一個加分點，同時也能事先想好自己在中英文面試時可能會被問到轉職問題的回答。就算在中英文面試時又被問到轉職問題，至少你現在寫自薦信的時候已經有準備了，答題時更能從容面對。

Lillian Tsai

10F-2,No.1, FuZhou St., Zhongzheng Dist., Taipei City 100,

Taiwan (R.O.C)

+886 2 2351 2007

XXXX@gmail.com

October 10, 2015　　　　　　　　　　　　　　　◀ 英文日期

Human Resource Manager　　　　　　　　　　　◀ 人力資源經理

XXXX Airlines　　　　　　　　　　　　　　　　◀ 航空公司

424, Section 2, Bade Road, Songshan

District, Taipei, Taiwan　　　　　　　　　　　◀ 航空公司英文地址

Dear Human Resource Manager,

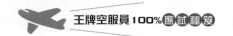
I am applying for the flight attendant position on your website. As a former flight attendant in XXX airlines, I have 2 years of flight attendant experiences. My consideration for my family is the main reason that I'd like to be a member of your team. My parents hope I can stay in Taiwan so that I can spend more time to accompany them. With my experience and being enthusiastic about the airline industry, I believe that I can be a great member of your team.

With 2-year overseas experiences, I have become more independent and have learned every nation has its own peculiar characteristics. Therefore, I can be more empathetic to passengers. I understand how excited and unsecure ones could be in the city when they have to communicate in unfamiliar languages. With these 2 years of flight attendant experiences in XXX airlines, I think I just can imagine this kind of feeling without any difficulties. I hope I can share and contribute my experience to your esteemed company.

I would like to have the opportunity to meet you in person to share more about my experiences and skills I would bring to your company. If you need any additional information, please contact me at +886 2 2351 2007 or XXX@gmail.com.

Thank you for your time and consideration.

Cordially,

Lillian Tsai

中文翻譯

　　人力資源經理您好，

　　我在貴公司網站上看到招聘空服員消息，在此想應徵該職務。我之前在 **XXX** 航空公司服務，有兩年的空服經驗。希望能成為貴公司一員的主要原因是我的家人，我的雙親希望我的派遣地能在台灣，這樣才能有多些時間陪伴他們。以我的經驗與對航空業的熱忱，我有信心能成為貴公司團隊的一員。

　　在國外生活的兩年，使我更加獨立，更能體會不同國家都有其特色，使我在空服工作中對旅客更有同理心。在語言無法完全溝通的異地，旅客興奮又帶著缺乏安全感的心情，在 **XXX** 航空公司任職兩年的空服員後，我相當能感同深受。我非常希望能在貴公司分享、貢獻這個在外地當空服的經驗，希望這份經驗能成為貴公司的資產。

　　希望能有機會與您面對面分享我的經驗，並能帶給貴公司的貢獻。若您需要任何額外的資訊，請以電話**+886 2 2351 2007** 或電子郵件信箱 XXX@gmail.com 與我聯絡。

　　謝謝您的時間與考慮！

誠摯地

Lillian Tsai

自薦信（Cover Letter）參考範例三

撰寫人背景說明

從本土航空公司轉外國航空公司的應試者。

從本土航空公司轉外國航空，一樣建議強調自己過往的空服經驗能為公司帶來的貢獻，因為這是你比其它沒有空服經驗的人強的優勢。但因為同樣是空服員工作，所以要轉換回本土航空公司，主考官最好奇的應該就是你的轉職理由。最容易被接受的轉職理由就是和派遣地相關的因素。你可以表示過去於任職期間曾停留過該航空公司的排遣地為由，表達出自己對這個派遣地的喜愛，甚至希望能住在那裡。但是你必須要寫出愛那個派遣地的實際例子，而不是風景美、治安好這些廣泛用詞；要想出實際例子就真的需要花點心思在你對派遣地的觀察，但這樣的心思對你是絕對有益處的，畢竟你之後真的有機會一直住在那城市，多了解以後要生活的地方對應試，或以後生活都是有正面的幫助的。

同樣的，與其讓主考官猜測你的轉職理由，不如就直接在推薦信上直接寫出轉職理由，直接解決主考官心中疑惑，能讓主考官覺得你有直接面對問題又了解人心的人格特質，這未嘗不是一個加分點，同時也能事先準備自己在中英文面試時可能會被問到轉職問題的回答。 就算在中英文面試時還是被問到轉職問題，至少你現在寫自薦信的時候已經有準備了，答題時更能從容面對。

Lillian Tsai ◀ 英文姓名

10F-2,No.1, FuZhou St.,

Zhongzheng Dist.,

Taipei City 100, Taiwan（R.O.C） ◀ 英文地址

+886 2 2351 2007 ◀ 聯絡電話

XXX@gmail.comDistrict, Taipei, Taiwan ◀ 電子郵件信箱

October 10, 2015 ◀ 英文日期

Human Resource Manager ◀ 人力資源經理

Cathay Pacific Airlines ◀ 國泰航空公司

8 Scenic Road, Hong Kong International

Airport, Lantau, Hong Kong ◀ 航空公司英文地址

Dear Human Resource Manager,

I am writing to express my interest in applying for the flight attendant position. Through my 3 years of experiences as a flight attendant in XXX airline, I have gained much from sharing with passengers. I believe my experience can contribute to your esteemed company.

The main reason that I want to be your team is I really love Hong Kong. I hope I can have an opportunity to serve in your company and live in Hong Kong.

The main reason why I want to contribute my flight experience to your team is not only that Cathy Pacific airlines is the great company, but also Hong Kong is my favorite city. I hope I can have more opportunities to have my breakfast in Hong Kong-style Teahouse. With my 3 years of flight attendant experiences, I fully understand the role of a flight attendant, including the challenges and trials. In addition to my love for Hong Kong, I am confident I am qualified for this position.

I look forward to the opportunity to speak with you further about the flight attendant position. If I can provide any further information, I can be reached at +886 2 2351 2007 or XXX@gmail.com.

Thank you for your time and consideration.

Respectfully,

Lillian Tsai

中文翻譯

人力資源經理您好，

得知貴公司正在招募空服團隊，我希望能成為貴公司團隊的一員。我在 XXX 航空有三年的空服員經驗，從和旅客分享的過程中學習到很多經驗。我相信我的經驗能為貴公司帶來貢獻。我想為貴公司效力的主要原因是我非常愛香港這個城市，我希望能有機會成為貴公司的團隊，能長住香港。

我希望能為貴公司效力，除了因為貴公司是很棒的航空公司外，也因為香港是我最愛的城市，我希望我能有更多的機會能在香港的茶餐廳吃早餐。在我過去三年的空服經驗中，我完全能理解空服員所要扮演的角色，包括面臨的挑戰與試煉。加上我非常愛香港，我有自信能符合貴公司對空服員的需求。

期待能有機會與您面談。若您需要任何額外的資訊，請以電話+886 2 2351 2007 或電子郵件信箱 XXX@gmail.com 與我聯絡。

謝謝您的時間與考慮！

尊敬地
Lillian Tsai

自薦信、履歷、自傳撰寫

④ 關於履歷表（Resume）、自傳（Autobiography）撰寫

　　在自薦信的部分說過如何為自己量身打造自薦信，而本篇的重點則是適用於為自己打造自傳的。基本上，除了履歷表上你就讀的學校、你曾任職過的公司是過去發生的事實，無法杜撰外，自傳也是能量身打造的。因為自傳和自薦信一樣，可以靠你自己的生活經驗找出與空服員工作最強的關聯性。

　　即使你要另外付費參加空服員補習班的自傳撰寫，也建議你能看完這個單元，並在看完這個單元後，試著思考一下該如何表達自己，替自己省下請人寫的金錢和時間。幫人撰寫自傳的自傳大師雖可以利用不同說法、不同語辭幫你美化你的自傳，但最開始也是需要你提供的自傳內容；還有就像偉人傳記一樣，即使請撰稿人代寫，撰稿人還是需要本人提供資訊是一樣的道理。也就是說，就算是再厲害的自傳大師，也需要你給予的資訊來豐富你的自傳。

　　所以這本書是教你如何撰寫自傳，而不是讓你直接照本宣科。想想職業別百百種，就算同樣的職業別，不同的環境與人生經歷也不能讓你將別人的自傳變成自己的。當然同樣的，如果你只想完成符合航空公司要求的一份自傳，且覺得照本宣科有幫助的話，那麼歡迎你使用本書的範例，並將範例替換成你的個人資料與經歷後，專屬於你的個人自傳就算完成了！

　　由於現在有許多男性也想走向空服之路，我在自薦信的單元中也舉了

程式設計師和空服員相互關聯性的例子。當然我沒做過程式設計師，只是憑自己的想像去思考之間的關聯性。我想表達的是，無論性別年齡、剛畢業或是要轉業、讀的科系相不相關，或之前的工作相不相關，只要你符合航空公司所規定的基本要求，都能寫出和空服員相關的自傳。雖然本書沒辦法像自傳聖經那樣，能讓讀者像查字典一樣，還列舉了各行各業轉空服員的自傳寫法；而且即便我能想出各行各業和空服員關聯性的自傳，但我沒有把握能比你真的從事那樣工作，有真實的經驗寫得好。與其這樣，我更希望我能用引導的方式，帶領你寫出自己最好的自傳，而且是主考官不管在自傳中找到什麼問題問你，你都能輕鬆自如的回答，我想這樣才真正能協助你達到成為空服員的夢想。

我知道人的本性就是求快、求好、求方便，但以我的自身經歷，自傳是真的沒辦法做到這樣，很多事情還是需要自己花心思的。自傳是你給主考官面試時的資料庫，是非常重要的，一定要在這裡花多一點的時間和心思。如果你的自傳寫的引人入勝，引發主考官的好奇心，那根本就不需要做中英文面試考前猜題了，因為你已經給了主考官想問的問題。

我一直強調自薦信和自傳必須包含你的親身經歷，因為這些經歷在你應試空服員的路上是非常重要的。所以放棄照本宣科吧！仔細想想自己擁有的特點與只有自己體會過的人生經驗，那才是對你最有幫助的。但在這裡要提醒你，主考官有時會從你的自傳中找問題發問。若你真的是照著別人的自傳，那至少要仔細研究一下別人的自傳內容。萬一別人在自傳中寫愛好園藝，但你卻一點也不了解，那就不只影響到自傳，而是影響到你的中英文答題了。

當然，我也在自薦信和自傳部分提供了實際範例給你參考。自薦信是自傳的濃縮，而自傳是自薦信的發揚光大。所以再次重申，無論你是男

生、女生，自薦信的三個範例——1.學校剛畢業沒工作經驗、2.從外商航空公司轉職到本土航空公司、3.從本土航空公司轉職到外商航空公司，你都能加上自傳部份的性格描述與性格實證來衍生為自傳。而自傳部份的實際範例也能成為自薦信的濃縮，可相互參考。

撰寫要點

1.可參考、但切勿抄襲。

坊間有許多中英文履歷／自傳範本可供參考，但請注意不要抄襲。因為你能找到的範本，其它應試者也能找到。主考官一次要看高達萬份的履歷表自傳，看到重複的機率很高，很容易疲乏。

2.個人資料簡明扼要

履歷表的主要目的是讓主考官以最快的方式認識你，在撰寫時請牢記。與其以花俏方式想引人注意，不如將個人資料條列清楚，讓主考官能以最快的速度了解你是否符合公司需求。

3.撰寫自傳的目的

自傳的目的是讓主考官了解你是否符合公司需求，並非身家調查。你家中有幾人、父母從事何種職業並不是重點，重點是讓主考官了解你有什麼特質能為公司效力，能為公司貢獻什麼。與其寫自己個性親切，不如舉出實例讓人看了自傳就覺得你是親切的人。當然像獨立、外向、應變能力強這些空服員很要求的特質，也不是你寫了就算。建議在撰寫時，將每個特質當作一個申論小題提出舉證，這樣的自傳才能深入人心，才是有價值的自傳。

4. 自傳貴精不貴多

通常航空公司會要求自傳字數，例如：**500 字**，請千萬不要超過。主考官需要在短時間內審查近萬份履歷表／自傳，在時間與精神的壓力下，真的沒有太多心思欣賞冗長的文章。

5. 先為自己做策略分析

回顧自己的優缺點和經歷，針對面試公司的企業文化列出自己的策略。例如：

- ✓ 面試動機
- ✓ 自己的優缺點
- ✓ 有什麼能讓人驚艷的地方
- ✓ 錄取你有什麼好處

策略擬定好之後再開始撰寫才容易寫出屬於你自己且能感動人的自傳。

6. 快速寫初稿再修改

建議你開始撰寫時不要想太多，以免越思考越下不了筆。先快速寫下初稿，有初稿後再進行修改，把贅字拿掉，將敘述字句潤飾地更簡潔。

7. 旁人建議很重要

完成後請旁人給建議，最好能有不同想法、不同性格的人給建議。因為你無法預期審查你履歷和自傳的主考官是什麼樣想法與性格的人。多聽幾個人的想法能讓你的自傳更符合不同閱讀個性的主考官。

1 應試前準備

2 應試技巧

3 飛上青空情境大模擬

自薦信、履歷、自傳撰寫
❺ 英文履歷、自傳實用字彙

以下列出幾個在履歷及自傳當中常會用到的字彙及例句，可以多加利用在履歷自傳上的撰寫。

1. attain vt 獲得、達到、完成

- I believe my painstaking to attain my goal in life is worthy.

  我相信我為了達成人生目標所付出的心力是值得的。

- I attain the honor of County Executive Award when I graduated from the elementary school.

  我在小學畢業時，獲得了縣長獎的榮譽。

2. achieve vt 實現、達成

- I believe that working hard will achieve my goal.

  我相信努力就能達成目標。

- I hope I can achieve all my objectives in my life.

  我希望我能達成我人生中所有目標。

3. accomplish vt 完成

- Whatever my wills are I may accomplish.

  我決心做的事都能完成。

- I think nothing can be accomplished easily in the world.

  我想世界上沒有任何事是能輕鬆完成的。

4. **assist** vt vi 協助

- I was a great helper to assist children in my neighborhood with anything they might need me.

  只要我鄰居的孩子們需要我的時候，我都會給予協助。

- Perhaps I could assist in some way?

  也許我能幫上忙？

5. **attitude** n 態度

- I have a positive work attitude.

  我具有積極的工作態度。

- My attitude towards this question is flexible.

  我對這個問題的態度是有彈性的。

6. **conduct** n 言行

- A man of irreproachable conduct commands the respect of others.

  品行端正的人受人尊重。

- My conduct is consistent with what I say.

  我的言行一致。

7. **concentrate** vt 專注

- I concentrated on community service.

  我專注在社區服務。

- I concentrated on studying Tang poems.

  我專注學習唐詩。

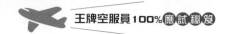

8. communicate vi 溝通

- I enjoy communicating with people from different countries.

  我喜歡跟來自不同國家的人溝通。

- Instead of making decisions alone, I like to communicate with people to seek for their opinions more.

  與其獨自作決定，我更喜歡與人溝通，尋求不同的意見。

9. determined adj 決心的；確定的

- My parents once asked me how I can be so determined that I am suitable for being a flight attendant.

  我的父母曾經問過我，我怎麼能如此確定自己適合空服員這個行業。

- I learned to be determined and not to give up.

  我學會了做事要下決心且不放棄。

10. focus vi 專注

- I like to try everything and always focus my mind on it.

  我喜歡嘗試所有事物，而且總是投注全部心力。

- We must focus on ourselves and respect other people.

  我們必須要專注於本身，同時尊重他人。

11. hope vt 希望

- I hope to achieve my dreams.

  我希望能實現我的夢想。

12. implement vt 實行

- The most important thing of fulfilling dreams is the ability to implement plans.

實現夢想最重要的是有實行計畫的能力。

13. inspire vt 啟發

- The noble example my teacher has set inspired me to seek for greater efforts.

  我的老師高尚的榜樣啟發我想更加努力。

- I hope I can inspire people.

  我希望我能啟發人們。

14. join vt 參與

- I joined the Dance Club when I was in the university.

  我在大學時參加舞蹈社。

- Will you join us in the discussion?

  你會參加我們的討論嗎？

15. manage vt 管理

- It was difficult but I managed to get it all done.

  雖然困難，但我還是完成了。

- I believe I can manage my life well.

  我相信我能好好安排我的人生。

16. prioritize vt 優先順序

- I have learned how to prioritize things in my life.

  我學會如何在生活中排出事情的優先順序。

- I have prioritized my career plan.

  我已經優先安排好我的職業生涯。

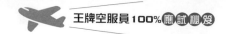
17. **qualify** [vi] 夠資格

- I qualified as a Chinese teacher since I passed the examination.

  我通過測試，取得了華語老師資格。

- I believe I will be qualified as a flight attendant.

  我相信我夠資格成為一位空服員。

18. **succeed** [vi] 成功

- My plan succeeded.

  我的計畫成功。

- I succeeded in getting the job.

  我成功的獲得工作。

19. **target** [n] [vt] 目標

- I have a great goal for my career.

  我對自己的職業生涯有遠大的目標。

- Our company has targeted children as our primary customers.

  我們公司將孩童作為主要顧客。

20. **worthy** [adj] 值得的

- worthy + of-N
- worthy + to-V
- The charities are worthy of our constant support.

  慈善事業值得我們持續支持。

- This is an event worthy to be remembered.

  這是一件值得回憶的事。

21. **value** n 價值

- I believe that everyone has different values.

  我想每個人都有不同的價值。

- The value of this work experience should be appreciated.

  這工作的價值應該被看重。

22. **obtain** vt 獲得、得到

- I will do all I can to obtain my dream job.

  我會盡全力得到我夢想中的工作。

- I believed that I can help people to obtain happy energy.

  我相信我能幫助人們獲得快樂能量。

23. **organize** vt 組織、安排

- I was honored to organize the graduation trip for my college classmates.

  我很榮幸為我的大學同學安排畢業旅行。

- I organized a photography club when I was in university.

  我在大學時成立了攝影社。

24. **vision** n 願景

- I have a clear vision of my future.

  我對我的未來有清楚的願景。

- When I was a child, I had a vision of being a flight attendant.

  小時候，我曾幻想自己是位空服員。

1 應試前準備

2 應試技巧

3 飛上青空情境大模擬

25. **ability** n 能力、才能

- I have the ability to keep calm in any emergency.

  我有在危急時保持冷靜的能力。

- Diligence compensates for the lack of ability.

  勤能補拙（勤勉能彌補自身能力不足）。

26. **goal** n 目標

- My goal in life is to help others.

  我的人生目標是幫助他人。

- This is the goal I am striving toward.

  這是我奮鬥的目標。

27. **independent** adj 獨立的

- Independent thinking is an absolute necessity for being a flight attendant.

  獨立思考是空服員所必須具備的。

- My parents always encourage me to be an independent person.

  我的父母總是鼓勵我成為獨立的人。

28. **influence** n 影響

- I like to listen to music. Listening to music has a calming influence on me.

  我喜歡聽音樂。聽音樂能讓我心情平靜。

- My parents have had a civilizing influence on me.

  我的父母對我有潛移默化的影響。

29. **become** vt 成為

- Nothing can weaken my resolve to become a flight attendant.

  沒有任何事能動搖我成為一名空服員的決心。

- My dream is to become a flight attendant.

  我的夢想是成為一名空服員。

30. **endeavor** n 努力

- Success comes from endeavors rather than being opportunistic.

  成功來自於努力而非機運。

- I believed that my constant endeavor will be valuable.

  我相信我持續的努力終將有價值。

下列的履歷範例是無論男女、無論你原先從事何種工作或剛從學校畢業都適用的。你會發現這些範例和其它你在網路上找到的英文自傳必備英語或中文自傳必寫句子不同，我是以引導式的方式讓你能寫出屬於你自己、與眾不同的履歷與自傳。

所以請你在看第 126～135 頁的範例時，想著套色字的重點，例如：

心胸開闊（性格特質描述）

和各國人士交談，接受各種不同文化差異（性格特質舉證）

在美式餐廳工作期間，因為自己在世界各地自助旅行訓練的英語能力與實際了解旅遊地人們的生活，所以許多來台工作或旅遊的外國人會為了來找我交談，特地來我們餐廳用餐。我會和他們分享一些關於台灣文化或旅遊的資訊和經驗，我常想這些和不同國籍人們分享的經驗，是我以後成為空服員與旅客相處的寶貴素材。（以實例強調自己的英語能力與世界觀，同時能應用於未來工作特點）

備註 切記描述後的舉證更重要。同時你人生中的實際經驗，才能讓你的自傳真實有生命力，能讓人像在看一個引人入勝的故事，而不是一份交差的自傳。

中文履歷表範例 1──無相關工作經驗者

應徵項目：空服員

陳淑芬
0933-221-XXX
XXX@gmail.com

【個人資料】

· 出生年月日：1988 / 04/ 12

· 身高：167 公分

· 體重：52 公斤

· 教育程度：輔仁大學大眾傳播系

· 語言能力：華語、台語、英語、日語

· 證照：美容師執照

· 興趣：閱讀、衝浪

【個人特點】

· 善於溝通　　　　　　· 樂觀進取

· 清晰的表達能力　　　· 平易近人

· 積極正面　　　　　　· 果決

【工作經歷摘要】

· （含產業／職稱／工作資歷共幾年／與應徵項目相關處等等。
例：在美妝產業擔任訓練講師一職近 4 年，美妝造型與溝通技巧
的專業使我有信心成為一位優秀的空服員。）

【工作經歷】（由近至遠）

· 公司名稱

· 倍斯特化妝品公司（2013 年 5 月至今）

· 職稱：訓練講師

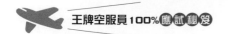
【工作內容】

- 新產品教育訓練
- 新人教育訓練
- 銷售技巧訓練
- 記者會支援
- 神秘訪客計畫執行
- 記者會支援

英文履歷表範例 1──無相關工作經驗者

CHEN,SHU-FEN (May Chen)
▲ 姓名

0933-221-XXX
▲ 行動電話號碼

XXX@gmail.com
▲ 電子郵件信箱

Objective: A challenging and career-oriented position offering increasing levels of responsibility and advancement and the opportunity to work for a quality organization.

【Personal】

- **Date of birth:** 1988/4/12
- **Height:** 167cm
- **Weight:** 52 kg
- **Education:** Mass Communication, Fu Jen Catholic University
- **Language:** Mandarin, Taiwanese, English, Japanese
- **License:** National Beauty Therapist License
- **Interests:** Reading, Surfing

【Highlights】

· Good communication skills

· Good presentation skill

· Positive attitude

· Optimistic and enterprising

· Approachable

· Decisive

【The summary of working experience】

Example: I have been worked as a trainer in cosmetic industry for 4 years. Professional knowledge in fashion style and communication skills gives me confidence to be an excellent flight attendant.

【Work Experience】(The latest one first)

· **Company name (Dates of employment):**

Company name Best International Taiwan Ltd. (May, 2013 to present)

· **Position:** Trainer

· **Responsibilities**

New Product Training

New Comer Training

Selling Skill Training

Press Conference Support

Mystery Shopper Project

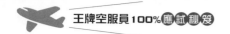

中文翻譯

目標：希望能貢獻一己之力，在卓越的公司中，擔任具有挑戰性與未來展望的工作。

【個人資料】

· 出生日期：1988/4/12

· 身高：167 公分

· 體重：52 公斤

· 教育程度：輔仁大學大眾傳播系

· 語言能力：華語、台語、英語、日語

· 執照認證：美容師執照

· 興趣：閱讀、衝浪

【個人特點】

· 善於溝通　　　　　　· 樂觀進取

· 清晰的表達能力　　　· 平易近人

· 積極正面　　　　　　· 果決

· **工作經歷摘要**：產業／職稱／工作資歷共幾年／與應徵項目相關處……
　等。

（例：在美妝產業擔任訓練講師一職近4年，美妝造型與溝通技巧的專業使我有信心成為一位優秀的空服員。）

【工作經歷】（由目前的工作開始）

· 公司名稱（起訖時間）：倍斯特餐廳（2013年五月至今）

· 職稱：訓練講師

【職務內容】

- 新產品教育訓練
- 新人教育訓練
- 銷售技巧訓練
- 記者會支援
- 神秘訪客計畫執行
- 記者會支援

中文履歷表範例 2——有相關工作經驗者

應徵項目：空服員

【個人資料】

- 出生年月日：1990/08/21
- 身高：178 公分
- 體重：71 公斤
- 教育程度：政治大學應用數學系
- 語言能力：華語、台語、英語
- 興趣：旅遊

林偉義
0921-568-XXX
電子信箱
XXX@gmail.com

【個人特點】

- 心胸開闊
- 謙虛
- 守時
- 體貼
- 隨和
- 勤奮

【工作經歷摘要】

- （含產業／職稱／工作資歷共幾年／與應徵項目相關處……等等。例：在美式餐廳擔任服務人員一職近 2 年，在顧客服務與餐點管理的經驗，使我有信心成為一位優秀的空服員。）

【工作經歷】（由近至遠）

・公司名稱

・Best Restaurant（2013 年 5 月至今）

・職稱：服務人員

・職務內容：

・顧客服務、餐點管理、客訴處理

英文履歷表範例 2──有相關工作經驗者

LIN, WEI-I (Brian Lin)

▲姓名

Mobile phone number:

0921-568-XXX

▲行動電話號碼

XXX@gmail.com

▲電子郵件信箱

Objective: A challenging and career-oriented position offering increasing levels of responsibility and advancement and the opportunity to work for a quality organization.

【Personal】

・**Date of birth:** 1990/08/21

・**Height:** 178 cm

・**Weight:** 69 kg

・**Education:** Mathematical Sciences, National Cheng Chi

University

· **Language:** Mandarin, Taiwanese, English

· **Interests:** Traveling

【 Highlights 】

· Open-minded

· Considerate

· Modest

· Easygoing

· Punctual

· Hardworking

【 The summary of working experience 】

Example:I worked as a waiter in the American restaurant for 2 years. With the experience of customer service and meals management, I have confidence to be an excellent flight attendant.

【 Work Experience 】(The latest one first)

· **Company name (Dates of employment):**

Best Restaurant (May, 2013 to present)

· **Position:** Waiter

· **Responsibilities**

Customer Service, Meal Management, Handling Customer Complaint

中文翻譯

目標：希望能貢獻一己之力，在卓越的公司中，擔任具有挑戰性與未來展望的工作。

【個人資料】

· **出生年月日**：1990/08/21

· **身高**：178 公分

· **體重**：69 公斤

· **教育程度**：政治大學應用數學系

· **語言能力**：華語、台語、英語

· **興趣**：旅遊

【個人特點】

· 心胸開闊　　　　　· 體貼

· 謙虛　　　　　　　· 隨和

· 守時　　　　　　　· 勤奮

· **工作經歷摘要**：產業／職稱／工作資歷共幾年／與應徵項目相關處……等。

（例：在美式餐廳擔任服務人員一職近 2 年，在顧客服務與餐點管理的經驗，使我有信心成為一位優秀的空服員。）

【工作經歷】（由目前的工作開始）

· **公司名稱（起訖時間）**：Best Restaurant（2013年5月至今）

· **職稱**：服務人員

【 職務內容】

· 顧客服務　　　　　· 餐點管理

· 客訴處理

中文履歷表範例 3──無工作經驗者

應徵項目：空服員

> 陳銘宜
> 0951-456-XXX
> XXX@gmail.com

【個人資料】

· 出生年月日：1992/02/02

· 身高：163 公分

· 體重：46 公斤

· 教育程度：師範大學中文系

· 語言能力：華語、台語、英語

· 興趣：攝影

【個人特點】

· 注重細節　　　　　　· 謹慎

· 負責任　　　　　　　· 熱忱

· 做事有彈性

【社團經驗摘要】

· （含社團名／職位／社團經歷共幾年／與應徵項目相關處……等等。例：在攝影社擔任公關 4 年，對台灣風景的了解與溝通技巧的專業使我有信心成為一位優秀的空服員。）

【社團經驗】（由近至遠）

【社團名稱】

· 攝影社（2013 年 5 月至今）

· 職位：公關

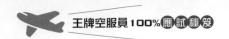

‧攝影社（2013 年 5 月至今）

‧職務內容：

‧推廣社務

‧爭取贊助

‧活動規劃執行

【實習經驗】（由近至遠）

‧ABC 公司（從 2014 年 5 月至 2015 年 5 月）

‧職稱：實習公關人員

‧職務內容：

‧協助公關經理籌劃公關活動

‧編輯與寄送週報給客戶

‧工作表現：

‧獲得最佳實習生獎

英文履歷表範例 3——無工作經驗者

Chen, Ming-Yi (Tina
Chen)

▲ 姓名

0951-456-XXX

▲ 行動電話號碼

XXX@gmail.com

▲ 電子郵件信箱

Objective: A challenging and career-oriented position offering increasing levels of responsibility and advancement and the opportunity to work for a quality organization.

【Personal】

· **Date of birth:** 1992/02/02
· **Height:** 163 cm
· **Weight:** 46 kg
· **Education:** Chinese Literature, National Taiwan Normal University
· **Language:** Mandarin, Taiwanese, English
· **Interests:** Photography

【Highlights】

· Detail–oriented
· Discreet
· Responsible
· Enthusiastic

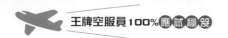
· Flexible

【 School clubs experience 】 (The latest one first)

· **School clubs name (Freshman , Sophomore, Junior, Senior)**

· **Example: Photo Club (Freshmen to Senior)**

· **Position: Public relations**

· **Responsibilities:**

Responsible for organizing events.

Mentored the new members.

· **Achievements:**

Organizing and executing inter-school photo event. 300 participants with satisfactory results.

【 Internship experience 】 (The latest one first)

· **Company name (Dates of employment)**

ABC Company (May, 2014 to May,2015)

· **Position: Public Relations Intern**

· **Responsibilities:**

Assistant PR manager in organizing a publicity program.

Edited and distributed weekly newsletter to clients.

· **Achievements:**

Obtained the award of best intern.

中文翻譯

目標：希望能貢獻一己之力，在卓越的公司中，擔任具有挑戰性與未來展望的工作。

【個人資料】

· 出生年月日：1992/02/02

· 身高：163 公分

· 體重：46 公斤

· 教育程度：師範大學中文系

· 語言能力：華語、台語、英語

· 興趣：攝影

【個人特點】

· 注重細節　　　　　　· 謹慎

· 負責任　　　　　　　· 熱忱

· 做事有彈性

【社團名稱】

· 攝影社（2013 年 5 月至今）

· 職位：公關

· 攝影社（2013 年 5 月至今）

【職務內容】

· 推廣社務、爭取贊助、活動規劃執行

【實習經驗】

· ABC 公司（從 2014 年 5 月至 2015 年 5 月）

· 職稱：實習公關人員

· 職務內容：協助公關經理籌劃公關活動、編輯與寄送週報給客戶

· 工作表現：獲得最佳實習生獎

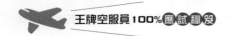
中文自傳範例 1——無工作經驗

　　蔡靈靈，今年剛從輔仁大學大眾傳播系畢業，評估自身的個性與能力後，選擇空服員為人生另一階段的開始。

　　樂於與人接觸的我（**性格特質描述**），從小跟家裡附近的商店都很熟，常常買東西變成幫老闆看店做生意，到現在也依然如此。對我而言，人不分親疏遠近，一樣用真誠對待。買舞鞋時看到老闆娘的孩子嘴破，我會馬上介紹自己常用藥給老闆娘，並分享嘴破的治療方法。（**性格特質舉證**）

空服員性格特質練習中文範例

獨立（性格特質描述）—自助旅行經歷（性格特質舉證）
細心（性格特質描述）—跟朋友用餐幫忙準備餐具面紙（性格特質舉證）
應變能力（性格特質描述）—水打翻了馬上處理（性格特質舉證）

　　在學期間，我在校園結識來自各個國家的朋友，以英語跟大家相處交談使我更能了解世界各地不同文化，跟不同文化背景的人都能輕鬆應對。（**以實例強調自己的英語能力與世界觀，同時能應用於未來工作特點**）

　　擔任攝影社公關期間，每年策畫與籌備與不同大專院校的攝影展活動。和不同學校的同學合作，使我學習到更多溝通方式，同時能很快與人熱絡。（**以實例敘述自己的社團經驗，同時能應用於未來工作特點**）

　　感謝您寶貴的時間，祝您今日愉快！

英文自傳範例 1──無工作經驗

　　My name is Lillian Tsai, graduating from Fu-Jen Catholic University, the Department of Mass communication. Evaluating my personalities and abilities, I choose to become a flight attendant as my new career.

　　I am easy-going individual,（性格特質描述）Ever since I was young, I have close relationships with neighbors. I often become a shop helper not a shopper. I bought dancing shoes another day and saw the boss's daughter was sick. I shared my therapy immediately. To me, people make no difference. I am greeting people with the same sincere attitude.（性格特質舉證）

空服員性格特質練習英文範例

Independent（性格特質描述）*-Travelling experience*（性格特質舉證）

Attentive（性格特質描述）*-Preparing tableware for friends*（性格特質舉證）

Resourceful（性格特質描述）*-Handling the situation of splitting water.*（性格特質舉證）

❶ 應試前準備

❷ 應試技巧

❸ 飛上青空情境大模擬

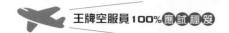

During the study period, I made friends and got along with everyone speaking in English. Thanks to those experiences, I've gained a better understanding of different cultures. Meanwhile, I firmly believe that once dealing with people of different backgrounds, I would know how to do my best in my future flight attendant career. （以實例強調自己的英語能力與世界觀，同時能應用於未來工作特點）

Acting as a PR in a photo club in the university, I planned for the photography exhibition activities with different universities every year. Through those experiences, how to communicate with different people and now I can get along with others immediately. （以實例敘述自己的社團經驗，同時能應用於未來工作特點）

Thank you for your time and hope you have a great day.

中文自傳範例 2──有工作經驗-美式餐廳服務員

　　蔡靈靈，輔仁大學大眾傳播系畢業，畢業後在美式餐廳工作，評估自身的個性與能力後，選擇空服員為人生另一階段的開始。

　　我樂於接受不同挑戰的我（**性格特質描述**），從大學開始就常一個人自助旅行，體驗各種不同的活動。我的旅行規劃並不是以去著名景點觀光為主，而是以體驗當地生活或參與特殊活動為目標。我曾為了嘗試高空彈跳與叢林飛行，一個人去清邁旅遊。每天上午參加一個活動，下午就在旅館對面的咖啡館與老闆娘聊天。這樣的行程安排不但符合我喜歡挑戰的性格，也能更了解清邁當地的文化。這種不畏挑戰與喜歡異文化的個性，讓我更確定自己適合空服員的工作。（**性格特質舉證**）

空服員性格特質練習中文範例

熱忱（**性格特質描述**）─主動幫助人（**性格特質舉證**）
謹慎（**性格特質描述**）─規劃自助旅行，食衣住行育樂每個環節謹慎規劃（**性格特質舉證**）
心胸開闊（**性格特質描述**）─和各國人士交談，接受各種不同文化差異（**性格特質舉證**）

　　在美式餐廳工作期間，因為自己在世界各地自助旅行訓練的英語能力與實際了解旅遊地人們的生活，所以許多來台工作或旅遊的外國人會為了來找我交談，特地來我們餐廳用餐。我會和他們分享一些關於台灣文化或旅遊的資訊和經驗，我常想這些和不同國籍人們分享的經驗，是我以後成為空服員與旅客相處的寶貴素材。（**以實例強調自己的英語能力與世界觀，同時能應用於未來工作特點**）

❶ 應試前準備

❷ 應試技巧

❸ 飛上青空情境大模擬

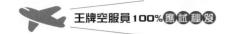

在美式餐廳擔任外場服務人員兩年工作，無論是顧客服務和餐點管理都累積相當經驗。只要有小孩一同前來的顧客，我一定會先給小孩鉛筆與畫冊，若鉛筆與畫冊發送完，我也會給小孩鉛筆和紙，讓小孩能有快樂的事專注，父母就能從容的點餐與用餐。所以我們餐廳在各分店中，帶著小孩前來的顧客比例是最高的。（以實例敘述自己的工作經驗，同時能應用於未來工作特點）

感謝您寶貴的時間，祝您今日愉快！

英文自傳範例 2——有工作經驗-美式餐廳服務員

　　My name is Lillian Tsai, graduating from Fu-Jen Catholic University, the Department of Mass communication. I worked for an American restaurant for 2 years. Evaluating my personalities and abilities, I choose to become a flight attendant as my future career.

　　I like challenges.（性格特質描述）Ever since I was in the university, I often travelled alone and experienced different activities. My travelling purpose is not visiting famous tourist spots. I like to experience local life and participate in special activities. For example, I went to Chiang Mai for bungee jumping and jungle flight. I participated in one activity every morning and stayed in a cafe in the afternoon. I enjoyed chatting with local people. I think this kind of personality can be an advantage of being a good flight attendant.（性格特質舉證）

空服員性格特質練習英文範例

Enthusiastic（性格特質描述）— *Helping people*（性格特質舉證）
Discreet（性格特質描述）—*Carefully planning to travel alone - including arranging all details.*（性格特質舉證）
Open-minded（性格特質描述）-*Communicate with people from other countries and enjoy different cultures.*（性格特質舉證）

　　My English ability and experiences of travelling alone have become my advantages when I worked in a American restaurant .

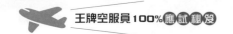
Many foreigners came to our restaurant for chatting with me. I will share what I knew about Taiwan and travelling information. I consider these sharing experiences will become my valuable materials if I become a flight attendant.（以實例強調自己的英語能力與世界觀，同時能應用於未來工作特點）

I worked as a waitress in an American restaurant for 2 years. During these 2 years, I've gained experiences from customer service and meals management. When parents with children came to the restaurant, I would give children drawing pencils and a drawing book. If I didn't have those on hand, I would give them papers instead. By doing this, I think parents can have time and pleasure to order and enjoy meals when children could have something focus on.（以實例敘述自己的工作經驗，同時能應用於未來工作特點）

Thank you for your time and hope you have a great day.

中文自傳範例 3──有工作經驗-護士

　　蔡靈靈，國立台北護理健康大學畢業，畢業後在台安醫院工作，評估自身的個性與能力後，選擇空服員為人生另一階段的開始。

　　喜歡與人分享生活經驗的我（**性格特質描述**），在醫院工作時，常常聽病患分享出國經驗。有慢性病的病患在分享出國經驗時，常常會表達自己在飛機上擔心病況的心情，畢竟飛機上的醫療資源有限。聽到他們的分享後，我開始想結合自己的旅遊興趣和護理專長，希望成為一位空服員，讓有慢性病的病患在搭乘飛機時能更自在。（**性格特質舉證**）

空服員性格特質練習中文範例

同理心（性格特質描述）─站在病患心情思考旅遊搭機（性格特質舉證）
細心（性格特質描述）─作為護士在工作上需要注意許多細節（性格特質舉證）
鎮定（性格特質描述）─在面臨病患發作時保持鎮定（性格特質舉證）

　　在決定選擇轉換人生職涯後，我就開始為自己成為一位空服員做準備。除了充實自己的英語能力外，也嘗試自己一個人出國自助旅行。從第一次自己出國自助旅行時的不安，到現在無論到哪個國家都能感到自在，讓我更有信心能勝任空服員這個工作。（**以實例強調自己的能力，同時能應用於未來工作特點**）

　　感謝您寶貴的時間，祝您今日愉快！

英文自傳範例3——有工作經驗－護士

My name is Lillian Tsai, graduating from National Taipei University of Nursing and Health Science. I worked as a nurse in Taiwan Adventist Hospital for 2 years. Evaluating my personalities and abilities, I choose to become a flight attendant as my future career.

I like sharing experiences with other people. （性格特質描述）My patients often shared their travelling experiences with me. Due to their having chronic diseases, they told me they usually would feel unsecure during flights. From that moment on, I've started to think about changing my career path. I would like to combine my interests and nursing ability by being a flight attendant, giving all passengers a sense of security. （性格特質舉證，同時與未來工作相關）

空服員性格特質練習英文範例

Empathy（性格特質描述） — *Put myself in the passengers' shoes to understand how unsecure patients might feel during the flight .*（性格特質舉證）

Attentiveness（性格特質描述）—*Being a nurse, I have an unusual ability to pay attention to details.*（性格特質舉證）

Stabilization（性格特質描述）—*Keep calm when facing the patient's disease onset*（性格特質舉證）

Since I've made up my mind, I've been preparing myself to

become a flight attendant. In addition to broadening my English ability, I start to travel alone. I still remember how worried I was when I travelled alone during the whole journey the first time. But now I feel at ease wherever I go. I am confident to be a good flight attendant .（以實例強調自己的能力，同時能應用於未來工作特點）

memo

PART 2 應試技巧

chapter 4　面試

① 面試要領

關於妝容

女生妝容

妝容——

　　離開空服員崗位後，我曾在 CHANEL、Christian Dior、LANCOME 等化妝品公司工作，大部分的時間是擔任教育訓練。對於妝容，依據我的經驗，就只有 6 個字——乾淨、立體、氣色。先做到這點，再考慮航空公司的文化，並參考該公司空服員的妝容來調整妝容風格。例如：華航、威航雖然是關係企業，但空服員文化與要求的特質完全不同，華航的制服是旗袍、威航的制服是 T 恤長褲，在妝容風格的表現上當然就不同。參加華航面試的妝容會是典雅，而參加威航面試的妝容則是亮眼。只要能做到整體妝容乾淨、立體與氣色，妝容風格就只是色彩的挑選和表現的小調整，一點都不難。這裡就告訴大家如何做到乾淨、立體與氣色。

乾淨——

　　底妝：想要一個乾淨的妝容，最重要的是選對適合你的底妝。很多女生追求白，所以在選擇底妝時，總是選比自己膚色白的。不但讓自己的臉和頸部變成兩個顏色，整個底妝看起來也變得灰灰髒髒的。其實選擇底妝，還要考慮自己是屬於冷色調或暖色調的膚色，像我就屬於暖色調的白皙，若選擇冷色調的白皙底妝就不是適合我了。聽起來很複雜嗎？其實就

是讓大家知道去購買底妝時要詢問的問題，因為在購買底妝時，詢問正確的問題很重要，之後就交給專業銷售人員為妳試顏色吧！

遮瑕：粉底產品不用多，在需要的地方做好遮瑕就可以有個自然薄透的乾淨妝容。遮瑕膏是我化妝包中必備物品，它的存在就像素描畫的橡皮擦，若下眼皮沾染到眼線或睫毛膏，只要先把它置於弄髒的地方，再用棉花棒輕輕一擦，馬上變回乾淨妝容。

立體：即使是輪廓深邃的歐美人士，也會在妝容上做出立體效果，所以立體是妝容很重要的部分。基本上很簡單，就是眉骨、Ｔ字部位打亮就可以了。當然如果要做到複雜點的，就利用深一色的粉底液及修容餅來打造吧！

氣色：腮紅和唇膏是打造氣色的關鍵。就我而言，我覺得腮紅格外重要。因為如果妳平常有做好唇部保養，唇色自然不會太差。但沒有了腮紅，氣色就會差很多。腮紅的畫法基本上依據臉型不同，沒什麼困難度。例如我是長型臉，所以腮紅就要平畫來增加臉的寬度。至於顏色選擇，只要和眼影與唇膏統一色調即可。不是說使用相同顏色，而是相同調性，即冷色調與暖色調。

就我個人而言，我覺得皮膚狀況是底妝好壞的重點。所以至少在面試前，請大家盡量吃好睡好，別抱持著僥倖心理，吃香喝辣的，如果皮膚出狀況，不但影響妝容，更影響心情，就得不償失囉！

其他

口腔氣味：除了妝容外，我覺得這點也非常重要。若你有抽煙習慣，除了口腔氣味，手部也會有香煙氣味。這部分也要注意。

指甲：建議指甲要修短並保持潔淨。若航空公司沒要求要擦指甲油，就別擦了。因為空服員是需要為旅客做餐點服務的，潔淨的短指甲會讓人有安全感。

香氛使用：雖然我個人非常喜愛香水的，還會依不同的天氣與服裝使用不同香水。但在面試時，我個人建議還是別使用香水吧！因為香氛是很個人化的，可能你很喜愛可是主考官很不喜歡，那就不太好了。

男生外在打理

若沒有突然的皮膚重大瑕疵，我建議就別上妝了。所以再回歸重點，就是請盡量吃好睡好，別讓皮膚出狀況。唯一的重點是眉毛，男生眉毛太淡或太少，確實會影響到氣色。所以稍微把雜亂的眉毛修整一下，眉毛太淡的話用女生乾掉的睫毛膏稍微補一點顏色，別用眉筆畫出太匠氣的眉毛會比較好。

服裝與髮型：自廉航加入與許多國外公司紛紛來台招考空服員後，因為航空公司變多，每家航空公司的文化不同，通常面試公司會依據公司文化與空服員制服，告知你該穿什麼樣的服裝與髮型參與面試，所以只要照做就行，沒什麼困難。大部分的航空公司招考仍是以套裝包頭為主，但威航則是要求穿著合身褲裝應試，同時還要求你搭配出最能表現個人主張的裝扮參與面試，要選出最活潑、有創意的空服員。所以請仔細詳讀航空公

司應考規定，再配合適宜妝容就行了。

　　我個人認為重點在於細節。服裝與鞋子的乾淨整齊度，頭髮的乾淨整齊，如果要作包頭的話，小小的細毛要用髮品收乾淨，這些是我覺得基本該做到的。

關於面試

　　面試時的題目包羅萬象，即使應試前做好萬全準備，背了一千題考古題，也總有可能應試題目不在你的考古題中。與其死背考古題，不如將自己的心態準備好。下列是你一定需要具備的：

- **應變能力**─培養應變能力的方法是，平常遇到任何狀況，絕不想著要找誰幫忙，而是立刻想到自己能怎麼解決。

- **平常心**─訓練平常心的方法是對自己有自信，相信自己能處理所有狀況。

- **冷靜**─訓練冷靜的方法是相信所有事情都能順利解決，無論現在看起來狀況有多糟糕。

- **笑容**─真誠的笑容需發自內心，培養自己對所有人事物抱持欣賞的心態。

- **眼神交會**─不要懼怕與人眼神交會，可先從親朋好友開始練習。

- **親和力**─時時抱持著為人著想的心情，看到旁人需要幫助，別想太多，直接釋出能協助的善意。

- **專注聽指令**─在吵雜慌亂的環境，也要靜下心專注在說話者的言談。不要邊聽邊想，這樣可能會聽了這一句，漏了下一句。平常訓練自己把別人的話聽完後再一起思考。

- **不東張西望**─只專注在自己身上，不過度關心身旁人的狀況。

- **不受外界影響**—外界的情緒與狀態可以參考，但不要影響到自己的狀況。

中英文 30 秒或 60 秒自我介紹

應試時，不一定會同時請你中英文自我介紹。但若同時請你中英文自我介紹時，請不要重覆介紹內容。你可把自我介紹想成以不同語言介紹你自己，而不是翻譯剛剛説過的話。

自我介紹和撰寫自傳不同，要説些能讓人印象深刻的事，最好是有畫面和溫度的故事。能引起人好奇心或觸動內心感受的自我介紹才能讓人記住你這個人。

千萬不要背誦別人的自我介紹，要花時間找出自己的特色，然後從自己的特色發展，這樣的自我介紹才能有溫度，讓主考官印象深刻。

中英文介紹重點

1.姓名

我在書中有舉我姓名的例子作為自我介紹的範例。你可能會説，因為你的名字真的很特別啊！是，我承認我的名字真的很特別，我也非常喜歡我的名字，但我相信沒有一個人對自己使用了二十年以上的名字沒有特別的感覺，即使你覺得自己的名字是菜市場名，在你使用這個名字的漫長歲月中，一定也有故事能分享，如果沒有的話，請問問幫你取名字的家人吧！我相信他們當初在幫你取名字的時候，一定有很多的想法和故事，這些都是你能拿來做介紹和分享的。我相信每個人的名字都有故事可以分享的，就算像我那麼特別的名字，其實我爸爸説是翻字典隨便選的呢！所以我相信你們的名字來源一定會比我特別。我真心覺得，用姓名做自我介紹

真的是一個很特別的切入點喔！

2. 學歷

我本身真的不太喜歡用學歷來做自我介紹的主軸，我個人覺得只要帶過就好。雖然名校出身的人會讓人一時刮目相看，肅然起敬，但我遇過名校出身的人，跟人交談時一直強調因為我是 XX 學校的，所以如何如何的，那給人的感覺真的不是很好。學歷固然能讓人了解你過去的努力，但重點是你所表現出來的人格特質，所以與其強調你是名校出身，不如以你在學時學到的，與空服員有關的部分發揮。

3. 引人注目的特點

因為沒見到你本人，所以沒辦法說出你引人注目的特點。不過在我空服員的生涯與之後做教育訓練所遇到的人當中，沒有一個人我說不出他引人注目的特點，所以我相信你一定比我能找出你自己引人注目的特點，因為每分每秒跟你相處的人只有你自己。有人看似安靜，其實喜歡搖滾樂。有人看似活潑，其實喜歡讀宋詞。不見得一定要跟人不同，只要你覺得是你的特點，你分享時就能生動感人。

4. 對應試工作的助益

這部分是綜合以上你對自己的了解，再連結到你選擇當空服員的動機，就能很快準備好了。要如何能讓內容吸引人注意，或更能讓人記住呢？很簡單，就是把自己的故事說得真實。相信我，你真實地說出自己的故事，比背再多別人的答案都更加令人動容。制式的答案聽起來雖然很漂亮，但沒有感情。空服員是個需要投入感情的工作，所以我鼓勵你說出自己真實的故事與感受，更何況空服員是個需要高應變能力的工作，如果你連面試的答題都沒自己的想法，請問主考官該如何相信你有能力去應變將來可能發生的所有狀況呢？

範例一

Track 01

介紹姓名、學歷、為什麼能成為一位好的空服員,是安全且一般應試考生會採用的方式。簡潔有重點,容易複製,但較無法令留下深刻印象。

Good morning. Everyone.

My Chinese Name is Tsai Ling Ling. You can call me Lillian. I just graduated from Fu Jen Catholic University. My major is Mass Communication.

I am here because I have confidence to be a great flight attendant. I am outgoing and independent, enjoying communicating with different people. When I was in the university, I joined the English Club and had friends from allover the

大家好,我是蔡靈靈。剛從輔仁大學大眾傳播系畢業。

今天會來參加面試是因為我有自信能成為一個好的空服員。我個性外向獨立,喜歡和不同人交往。我在大學時,參加了英語社,認識了來自世界各地不同的朋友。也因為如此,了解了各

world. I experienced a great variety of cultures and believe those experiences can make a good contribution to my flight attendant career.

It was a great pleasure to present myself here. I hope I will have an opportunity to become a member of your team.

Thank you for your time and hope you have a great day.

國不同的文化，相信這樣的經驗能對未來的空服工作有很大的幫助。

我很榮幸能有和您面試，希望能有機會成為貴團隊的一員。

感謝您寶貴的時間，祝您今日愉快！

① 應試前準備

② 應試技巧

③ 飛上青空情境大模擬

範例二

Track 02

介紹姓名後，講一個只有自己知道的故事，並且是能和成為一位優秀空服員有關的故事。這需要花時間思考，不能複製任何書上或別人跟你說的重點，但絕對會有溫度，並令人留下深刻印象。

Hello, everyone. My Chinese name is Tsai Ling Ling. You can call me Lillian. The stroke count of my Chinese name is 65. I haven't met anyone who gets more strokes in his or her name than I do. Therefore, my Chinese name always can impress people. I think I have a special name as well. So now, I would like to share my name story today.

Because of this special Chinese name, I often became the first one to be noticed in schools or in groups.

大家好，我是蔡靈靈，靈是靈魂的靈，比劃很多，有 65 劃。我從來沒看過其它人的名字筆劃比我多的，所以從小到大，我的名字都能讓人印象深刻。我也覺得自己有個特別的名字，所以今天的自我介紹想和大家分享我的名字。

因為名字被特別注目的關係，所以無論在學校或陌生團體中，我常常是最先被審視的。

Somehow as time has gone by, I have had high expectations for myself since I was a little girl. Like, I never cried when I fell because I didn't want get embarrassed in front of others. I'm strong-willed, and believe that I can do everything well.

I'm an outgoing person and I think this personality is perfect for being a flight attendant, especially when flight attendants have to face a variety of people and handle different situations. They also need to be strong-willed and confident as well. And I believe I have possessed these two qualities, which help me to stand out and become a competent flight attendant.

Thank you for your time and hope you have a great day.

不知不覺，隨著時間，從小到大我對自我要求都特別高，什麼事都要做到最好，就算跌倒也不哭，因為我不想在他人面前丟臉。這樣的性格，讓我擁有堅強的意志和求好的心態，同時相信自己什麼事都做得到。

我是個外向的人，我想這樣的的性格非常適合空服員的工作，尤其空服員每天面對不同的人，處理不同的狀況，他們還需要堅強的意志和自信。而我也相信我擁有這兩項特質，讓我能夠有出眾的表現、成為有能力的空服員。

感謝您寶貴的時間，祝您今日愉快！

1 應試前準備

2 應試技巧

3 飛上青空情境大模擬

範例三

Track 03

介紹姓名後，講一個自己喜歡的興趣，並且是能和成為一個優秀空服員有關的興趣。這樣的自我介紹能引起共鳴，也能給人留下與眾不同印象。

Hello, everyone. My Chinese name is Tsai Ling Ling. You can call me Lillian. Today, I would like to take this opportunity to share a great thing with you. That is origami.

I personally enjoy origami so much as I can make origami papers anytime and anywhere. When I wait for someone or feel upset, making origami papers can comfort me. That's why I always have origami papers with me.

I think the awesome part of origami is that it is an interest that can be shared. I like to share things with people. I often give out my origami

大家好，我是蔡靈靈，今天的自我介紹想與大家分享我的興趣－摺紙。

會喜歡摺紙是因為摺紙不需要特別場地，是隨時隨地都能摺的，無論是等人的時候或是覺得心煩的時候，摺紙都能安定我的心情，所以我的隨身包包中一定會有色紙。

我覺得摺紙吸引我的地方不只這些，最棒的是摺紙是可以分享的。我是個很喜歡分享的人，常常會將自己

works to other people, not only to my friends, but also to children seated next to me in a restaurant. They are happy to receive them.

I have my origami papers in my bag as well and hope to have an opportunity to share them with you.

Thank you for your time and hope you have a great day.

摺的星星或紙鶴這些作品，分送給身邊的人。不一定是朋友，有時也會送給餐廳隔壁桌的小朋友，大家都非常喜歡。

今天的隨身包裡當然也有色紙，希望也有機會跟大家分享。

感謝您寶貴的時間，祝您今日愉快！

❶ 應試前準備

❷ 應試技巧

❸ 飛上青空情境大模擬

範例四

Track 04

介紹姓名後，講一個自己喜歡的運動，並且是能和成為一個優秀空服員有關的運動。這樣的自我介紹能引起共鳴，也能給人留下與眾不同印象。

Hello, everyone. My Chinese name is Tsai Ling Ling. You can call me Lillian. Today, I would like to take this opportunity to share my favorite exercise with you. That is jogging.

I personally enjoy jogging because there is no venue and time limitation. I often travel alone and go jogging in the afternoon around hotels. When I get tired, I will find a restaurant to take a rest and have my dinner. I enjoy this kind of travelling very much, from which I have gained confidence that I can be a great flight attendant since I've learned to quickly get used to staying

大家好，我是蔡靈靈，今天的自我介紹想與大家分享我喜愛的運動－慢跑。

會喜歡慢跑是因為不需要特別場地，在家附近就可以跑；出國旅遊的時候也可以跑。因為我都是一個人自助旅行，所以常會在下午的時候在飯店附近慢跑，跑累的時候就找一家餐館休息一下，準備吃晚餐。我很享受這樣一個人的旅行，並從這樣的旅行獲取成為優秀空服員的自信，因為我學會習慣待在任何國家，享受並欣賞

in any country, enjoy and appreciate different living styles at ease. I think those experiences help me develop essential qualities of an excellent flight attendant.

Jogging can release stress, help me to concentrate and inspire me to see many things and have great ideas I might not notice and have in my life. Moreover, jogging doesn't have time limitation. From my personal experience, I highly recommend jogging to you.

Thank you for your time and hope you have a great day.

不同的生活方式。我想這些經驗都有助於我累積身為一位空服員需要具備的特質。

慢跑能讓我釋放壓力，集中精神，看到許多平常看不到、得不到的東西，而且慢跑沒有時間限制。以我個人的慢跑經驗，真的覺得是個很棒的運動，想推薦給大家。

感謝您寶貴的時間，祝您今日愉快！

範例五

Track 05

介紹姓名後，介紹自己喜歡的一本書，並且是能和成為一個優秀空服員有關的一本書。這樣的自我介紹能引起共鳴，也能給人留下與眾不同印象。

Hello, everyone. My Chinese name is Tsai Ling Ling. You can call me Lillian. Today, I would like to take this opportunity to share my favorite book with you-*The Little Prince*.

The novella is the 3rd most-translated book in the world and was voted the best book of the 20th century in France. This book inspired me in many aspects. It even inspired me to be a flight attendant. I enjoy travelling with this book to different countries. Every country has its unique atmosphere and culture. I often think every city is just like one planet, I hope I have opportunities to see them all.

大家好，我是蔡靈靈，今天的自我介紹想與大家分享我喜愛的書—《小王子》。

這本書是全世界第三本被廣泛翻譯的書，同時是二十世紀法國票選最佳書籍。這本書在很多方面激勵我，同時也讓我想成為一位空服員。我喜歡跟小王子一起到不同的國家，而每個國家都有獨特的氛圍和文化。我覺得不同的城市就像不同的星球，我希望能有機會看遍所有城市。

The Little Prince is a great book for everyone, especially for a flight attendant. Being a flight attendant means you might have lots of time being alone in other countries. Through this book, we will use different points of view to see the world and life.

Thank you for your time and hope you have a great day.

《小王子》這本書對每個人來說都會是一本很棒的書，尤其是對空服員而言。空服員有許多時間會獨自在其它國家，透過這本書，我想能用不同的觀點看世界與生活。

感謝您寶貴的時間，祝您今日愉快！

範例六

Track 07

介紹姓名後，介紹自己的座右銘，並且是能和成為一個優秀空服員有關的座右銘。這樣的自我介紹能引起共鳴，也能給人留下與眾不同印象。

Hello, everyone. My Chinese name is Tsai Ling Ling. You can call me Lillian. Today, I would like to take this opportunity to share my motto with you-Happiness depends on what you give not on what you get.

大家好，我是蔡靈靈，今天的自我介紹想與大家分享我的座右銘—快樂來自於給予，而非獲得（施比受更有福）。

I was a person who wanted to pursue everything in my life. I thought happiness was to own the things I want. By chance, I saw the report about a young man who devotes himself to taking care of children in remote areas. I saw a great smile on his face when he bought new slippers for the children. I was so touched at that moment. Since then, I have always been thinking about this motto—Happiness depends on what you give not on what you get.

This motto leads me here. Meanwhile, I always think about how to use my ability to contribute. I find out being a flight attendant will be my destiny. I can give more in this career than others. I really hope I can have an opportunity to put the idea of this motto into practice.

Thank you for your time and hope you have a great day.

我以前是個在生活中愛好追求的人，我總認為快樂就是來自於我擁有想要的東西。偶然的一次機會，我看到一個照顧偏遠地區孩童的年輕人報導。他在買新拖鞋給孩子們的臉上，有著非常棒的笑容，讓我非常感動。從那刻起，在生活中我總是會想起這句話，快樂來自於給予，而非獲得（施比受更有福）。

這句話也引領我今天來到這裡。我在思考自己能以什麼方式為世界貢獻己力時，我發現成為一位空服員就是答案，在這裡我能貢獻的，比在其他的地方還多。我希望能有機會在這裡實現自己的座右銘。

感謝您寶貴的時間，祝您今日愉快！

給大家一些座右銘作為參考，請盡情發展成自己的故事吧！

Nothing is possible for a willing heart.

只要有心，沒有不可能的事。

All things are difficult before they are easy.

所有事都是先難後易。

God helps those who help themselves.

天助自助者。

If a thing is worth doing it is worth doing well.

如果一件事是值得做的，那就值得把這件事做好。

Actions speak louder than words.

行動比說更有力量。

One today is worth two tomorrows.

一個今天，勝過兩個明天（把握今日）。

Take one's courage in both hands.

勇往直前。

Haste makes waste.

欲速則不達。

Every man is his own worst enemy.

最大的敵人就是自己。

③ 中英文短文朗讀技巧

在面試時，主考官為了能了解你的聲音魅力，通常會請應試者唸一段短文，短文的內容多元化，但大家其實不用擔心內容，只要你平常做好準備與勤加練習，什麼樣的內容都難不倒你。下面為你整理了一些注意事項，建議大家平常在閱讀任何文字時，都能唸出來，剛開始可以先把自己的聲音錄起來，除了自己聽之外，可以請旁人給意見。只要多加練習，任何文章交到你手裡，你就能自然而然朗讀出來。當然如果你想事半功倍，就找與空服員有關的內容做朗讀。例如：廣播詞或航空公司雜誌。

注意事項

● 音量控制

音量適中，不刻意放大聲量，也不能有氣無力。請旁人評估自己平時說話音量做調整，同時注意不要因緊張而聲音抖動。

● 語調抑揚頓挫

切記語調勿矯揉做作，不刻意模仿。但要做到這點，需要練習。沒有人天生說話就有感情，就有抑揚頓挫，但只要專注練習，每個人都能做得很好。

平時多將文章讀出聲音並錄音檢視。讀文章時投注情感，聽起來很抽象，但其實不難。以英文為例，疑問句的尾音要上揚就是最自然的抑揚頓挫。想想剛開始學英文時，遇到疑問句時都故意將尾音上揚，聽起來很奇

怪，讀起來很彆扭。但經過一段時間，習慣就變自然了。

　　剛開始練習讀文章時，先預讀文章，在文章上將語調上升、下降、停頓、轉折等高低起伏先做記號，讀文章的時候將這些語調記號誇張地表現出來，多讀幾遍，一直讀到能自然表現出語調為止。

● 咬字清楚

　　每個人都不同的咬字問題需要注意。找出自己的咬字問題，專注解決自己的問題，不需要重新練習每個咬字重點。

　　以中文而言，像ㄅ／ㄥ、ㄖ／ㄌ、ㄢ／ㄤ、ㄜ／ㄡ、ㄗ／ㄓ、ㄙ／ㄕ以及ㄓ／ㄗ／ㄖ等捲舌音要特別注意。

　　以英文來說，長短母音分清楚-例如：lack/ lake、made/mad、sake/sack、snack/snake 注意單字重音-例如：dessert/desert。劃分單字音節幫助記憶-音節以單字中母音數目為計算，分為單音節、雙音節與多音節（三個以上母音）。劃分方法是先找母音後找子音。

● 注意語速

　　語速不急不徐，寧可慢不要快，務必每句話都能讓人聽清楚。

準備方法

　　找出自己發音缺陷，加強練習、每天朗讀文章，錄音確認。英文廣播詞是很好的練習內容，除了本書會提供你一些英文廣播詞範本，目前網路上也有一些英文廣播詞有聲網站，幫助你練習。但在此不列出網址，因為不確定當你閱讀本書時，這些網站是否仍存在，不過，其實只要你將本書提供的廣播詞練熟，就不會有問題囉！

A

◉ arrival 入境

We are waiting for the arrival of the next flight.

我們在等下一班入境航班。

◉ Animal & Plant Quarantine 動植物檢疫

If you bring your dog to Korea, you must submit a healthy certificate to the animal quarantine officer at the port of entry.

如果你要帶你的小狗去韓國，你必須在入韓國時將小狗的健康證明交給動物檢疫人員。

◉ airsick 暈機／airsickness Bag 嘔吐袋

If you are prone to get airsick, please take a airsickness bag with you.

如果您會暈機，請隨時帶著嘔吐袋。

◉ aisle seat 走道座位

Could I have an aisle seat, please?

請給我走道座位。

◉air traffic congestion　航路擁擠

The flight will be delayed due to air traffic congestion.

由於航路擁擠，班機將會延誤。

◉armrest　扶手

For your safety, please hold an armrest when you are at lavatory.

為了您的安全，當您在洗手間時，請握住扶手。

◉altitude　高度

We will start to provide drinks when we are flying at an altitude of 10,000 feet.

當我們飛航至 10,000 英呎高度，將會開始供應飲料。

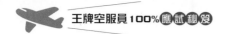
B

◉ baby nursing room 哺乳室

Nowadays, most airports have baby nursing rooms.

現在大部分的機場都有哺乳室。

◉ boarding gate 登機門

The boarding gate is crowded.

登機門擠滿人群。

◉ baggage 行李／**free baggage allowance** 行李重量限制

What is the free baggage allowance of this airline?

這家航空公司的行李限重是多少？

◉ baggage delivery 行李託運服務

Enjoy the baggage delivery service of ABC airline.

歡迎使用 ABC 航空的行李託運服務。

◉ check-in baggage 託運行李

For flight safety, please leave your scissors in your check-in baggage.

為了飛航安全，請將你的剪刀放置在託運行李中。

◉ baggage claim area 行李提領區

Excuse me, where is the baggage claim area?

請問行李提領區在哪裡？

◉baggage carousel　行李運輸帶

Don't panic. Your baggage is still on the baggage carousel.

別驚慌。你的行李還在行李運輸帶上。

◉baggage (luggage) tag　行李標籤

To prevent your baggage from getting lost, it might be better for you to keep your baggage tag.

最好保留你的行李標籤，避免行李遺失。

◉bonded baggage　存關行李

You will not get your bonded baggage until you pay the duty.

除非您將關稅結清，否則您拿不到您的存關行李。

◉baby bassinet　嬰兒床

Baby bassinets and packs as well as a wide range of baby food are available during the flight. Please feel free to ask from the flight attendants if necessary.

班機途中我們都有提供嬰兒床、嬰兒用品與多樣化嬰兒食品。若有需要，歡迎詢問我們的空服員。

◉blanket　毛毯／pillow　枕頭

May I have an extra blanket (pillow)? Thank you.

可以多給我一條毛毯／一塊枕頭嗎？謝謝！

1 應試前準備

2 應試技巧

3 飛上青空情境大模擬

◉boarding pass 登機證

Please get your passport and boarding pass ready.

請準備好您的護照與登機證。

◉boarding gate 登機門

Your boarding gate is No.5.

您的登機門是五號。

◉boarding time 登機時間

Please pay attention to your boarding time. Thank you.

請留意您的登機時間,謝謝。

◉body temperature scanner 溫度檢測儀

You need to go through the body temperature scanner at the airport.

在機場,您需要通過溫度檢測儀。

◉briefing 任務簡介／crew 組員

Flight crew will attend a briefing meeting before every flight.

每趟飛行前,飛行組員都要參與任務簡介會議。

◉buckle 扣環

It's much safer if you buckle up during the flight.

當您在飛機上,繫好安全帶會安全得多。

◉bracing position　前抱臥姿／ditching　水上迫降

In an emergency ditching, you should keep your brace position until the aircraft comes to a complete stop.

緊急水上迫降時，請保持前抱臥姿直到飛機完全停止。

memo

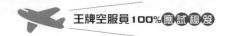
C

◉ cabin class 飛機艙等／first class 頭等艙／
business class 商務艙／economic class 經濟艙

Airlines offer different cabin classes for travelers to
choose from. You can choose first class, business class or economic
class based on your budget.

航空公司為旅人提供不同艙等，您可以根據您的預算選擇頭等艙、商
務艙或經濟艙。

◉ call button 呼叫鈕／flight attendant 空服員

If you need a flight attendant for any assistance, just press the call
button.

如果您需要空服員任何協助，只要按呼叫鈕。

◉ captain 機長

The captain will inform all the information you need when he
makes an announcement.

機長將會在廣播中告知您所需要的資訊。

◉ check-in counter 報到櫃台

Passengers should check in first at check-in counter 2 hours before
your flight departs.

旅客應在飛機起飛前兩小時先至報到櫃台報到。

◉car rental service 租車服務

You can arrange car rental service in advance when you travelling abroad.

出國時，您可以事先安排租車服務。

◉Carry-on baggage is subject to inspection. 手提物品接受檢查

Carry-on baggage is subject to inspection. It is mandatory.

手提物品接受檢查是強制性的。

◉cart return area 手推車回收處

Please return your cart to the cart return area.

請將手推車放置到手推車回收處。

◉cellular phone service 行動電話聯合服務台

You can charge your mobile phone at the counter of cellular phone service. 您的手機可以在行動電話聯合服務台充電。

◉charter flight 包機

Is this a regular flight or a charter flight?

這是正常航班還是包機航班？

◉window seat 靠窗座位／aisle seat 走道座位／

center seat 中間座位

Would you prefer a window, an aisle, or a center seat？

請問您想要靠窗、走道或中間的位置？

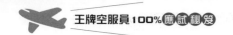
◉ **customs service counter** 海關服務櫃台

You can get the information you need at the customs service counter.

您可以在海關服務櫃台得到你所需要的資訊。

◉ **control tower** 塔台

Every plane has to wait for the go-ahead from the control tower.

每架飛機都必須等待塔台的起飛信號。

◉ **connecting passenger** 轉機旅客

Connecting passengers should pay attention to transit time.

轉機旅客需注意轉機時間。

◉ **connecting flight** 接駁班機

I am afraid I might miss my connecting flight.

我擔心我會錯過我的接駁班機。

◉ **confirmation** 確認

The price is subject to our confirmation.

價格經我們確認後生效。

◉ **courtesy bus** 免費接駁巴士

A courtesy bus operates between the airport and the downtown.

免費接駁巴士來往於機場與市區間。

◉ carry-on bag (hand baggage) 手提行李

How many pieces of hand baggage do you have?

您有多少件手提行李？

◉ currency declaration 貨幣申報／customs 海關

You might need to show your currency declaration to customs.

您可能需要在海關處出示貨幣申報。

◉ control panel 座位把手上控制面板

You can change your music channels via the control panel.

您可以在座位把手上控制面板選擇您的音樂頻道。

◉ customs duty payment/ pay customs duty 海關課稅

Some special articles need customs duty payment./ You should pay customs duty for some specific articles.

一些特別的物件需要在海關課稅處付特定稅率。

◉ complimentary 免費

Those are our complimentary beauty products for you.

這是我們為您準備的免費護膚品。

◉ customs inspection counter 海關檢查櫃台

Where is the customs inspection counter?

請問海關檢查櫃台在哪裡？

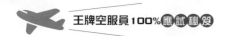
D

◉ **demonstration** 示範

Flight attendant will give you the safety demonstration shortly.

空服員很快將為您做安全示範。

◉ **departure tax (airport tax)** 機場稅

Departure tax is included in the ticket price.

機場稅包含在機票裡面

◉ **departing passenger** 出境旅客／

immigration inspection 出境檢查

All departing passengers are required to proceed to the customs and immigration inspection.

所有出境旅客需通過海關的出境查驗。

◉ **foreign currency exchange** 外幣兌換／**duty free** 免稅店／

departure (hall/ lobby) 出境大廳

Foreign currency exchange and duty free shops are available at the international departure hall.

在國際航站出境大廳有外幣兌換與免稅店。

◉ **delay** 延誤

I owe you an apology for the delay.

為了這次的延誤向您道歉。

◉ destination　目的地

Where is your destination?

請問您的目的地在哪？

◉ diaper　尿布

Do you need extra diapers for your baby?

請問您需要額外的尿布嗎？

◉ disabled customer service counter　無障礙服務台

elevator for the disabled　身心障礙電梯

restroom for the disabled　身心障礙廁所

Our ground staff will show you the way to the disabled customer service counter. 我們的地勤人員會帶您去無障礙服務台。

◉ dispatch office　派遣室

Flight attendants will get their monthly schedule from the dispatch office. 空服員會從派遣室拿到每月班表。

◉ departure　出境

A board inside the airport shows arrivals and departures.

機場內的顯示幕有飛機出境與入境資訊。

◉ domestic terminal　國內線航廈

Be careful! Don't mix up the international terminal and domestic terminal. 小心！別把國際線航廈與國內線航廈搞混囉！

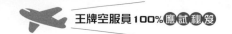

◉duty-free catalog 免稅商品目錄／safety card 安全手冊／
headsets 耳機

You will find your duty-free catalog ,safety card and headsets in front of your seat. 在您的座位前有免稅商品目錄和安全手冊。

◉dry chemical extinguisher 乾粉滅火器

Every flight attendant knows how to use a dry chemical extinguisher. 每位空服員都知道如何使用乾粉滅火器。

◉dutiable goods 課稅商品

Don't try to cheat the customs by not declaring dutiable goods.
別試著瞞騙海關不申報課稅商品。

◉declaration form 申報表格

Could you give me a customs declaration form, please?
請給我一份海關申報表格？

◉duty-free items 免稅商品

Where do I pick up duty free items I bought?
請問我要去哪裡拿我買的免稅商品？

E

◉ embarkation card　登機卡

Please write all the information in English on your embarkation card.

請用英文在入境卡寫下所有資訊。

◉ emergency　急救

It is important to stay calm in any emergency situations.

在任何緊急狀況下保持冷靜是重要的。

◉ emergency exit　逃生出口

Flight attendants will show you the nearest emergency exit in a safety demonstration. Please pay attention to it.

空服員在安全示範時會告訴您最近的逃生出口，請留意。

◉ escalator　自動扶梯／lift　電梯

If you need to go upstairs, please take the escalator or the lift there.

若您要上樓，請搭那邊的自動扶梯或電梯上樓。

◉ estimated time of arrival (ETA)　預計到達時間

　 estimated time of departure (ETD)　預計起飛時間

When is the estimated time of arrival (departure)?

請問預計到達／起飛時間是什麼時候？

◉ evacuate 疏散／evacuation on land 陸上逃生

All passengers must be evacuated in 90 seconds if the evacuation occurred on land.

迫降時，所有旅客需在 90 秒內疏散。

◉ exchange rate 匯率

The exchange rate today is 3.77 Japanese yen to the 1 NT dolloar.

今天的匯率是 1 元新台幣換 3.77 日幣。

◉ eye shade 眼罩／socks 襪子／tooth brush 牙刷／tooth paste 牙膏／comb 梳子／travel kit 航空盥洗包／long haul flight 長程航班

An eyeshade, socks, a tooth brush, a tooth paste, and a comb will be prepared in a travel kit if you travel with the first class and business class for a long haul flight.

若搭乘頭等艙或商務艙的長程航班，眼罩、襪子、牙刷、牙膏、梳子會在航空盥洗包中。

F

● facilities and services directory 設施服務指南

When you are at the airport, make sure check the facilities and services directory first.

當您在機場時，記得先查看設施服務指南。

● flight information board 航班顯示板

You can find your continuing flight information on the fight information board.

您可以在航班顯示板找到您接續航班的資訊。

● forced landing 迫降

Due to engine trouble, the plane had to make a forced landing.

由於機械因素，飛機必須進行迫降。

● fasten seat belt 扣安全帶／seat belt 安全帶

Please fasten the seat belt whenever you are seated.

在座位上請繫好安全帶。

● footrest 腳踏板

Please restore your footrest to its original position when the flight takes off.

在飛機起飛時，請將您的腳踏板收起。

G

◉ **galley** 廚房

Every aircraft is equipped with a multifunction galley.

每架飛機都配備有多功能廚房。

◉ **gate number** 登機門號碼

The boarding gate of the flight is at gate number 5.

班機在五號登機門登機。

◉ **goods to declare** 報關物品

Do you have any goods to declare for customs?

請問您有任何報關物品嗎？

◉ **ground staff (crew)** 地勤人員

If you will continue the flight with us, please obtain your boarding pass from the ground staff and wait for departure in the terminal.

若您將繼續我們的航班，我們地勤人員會給您登機證，請您在航廈中等候起飛。

H

◉ handicapped passenger 殘疾旅客

Handicapped passengers might require our extra attention during the flight.

在飛航期間，殘疾旅客需要我們額外注意。

◉ headwind 逆風

We are now flying against a headwind.

我們現在正逆風飛行。

◉ hotel and limousine service center 旅館與接車服務中心／hotel information center 旅館服務台

You can get the hotel information in the hotel and limousine service center.

你可以在旅館與接車服務中心獲得資訊。

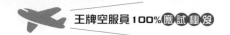
I．J

◉ immigration card (form) 入境表格

Would you care for an immigration form?

請問您需要入境表格嗎？

◉ immigration control 出入境檢察

Every passenger must pass the immigration control at the airport.

在機場，每位旅客都必須接受出入境檢查。

◉ infant 嬰兒

If you are travelling with an infant for the first time, you can consult flight attendants for their advice on how to take care of an infant during the flight.

如果您第一次帶嬰兒旅行，您可以詢問空服員在飛機上照顧嬰兒需要注意事項。

◉ in-flight shopping 機上購物

in-flight sales 機上免稅品販售

In-flight shopping offers you a chance to purchase in-flight sales such as your favorite brands with great prices.

您可以在機上購物買到您喜愛又免稅的品牌。

◉ in-flight entertainment system 機上娛樂系統

Low cost airlines do not provide in-flight entertainment system.

Remember to bring your favorite books with you.

廉航不提供機上娛樂系統，記得帶你喜歡的書。

◉immigration office　出入境辦公室

You can go to the immigration office for travel document applications.

你可以去入出境辦公室辦理旅行證件。

◉information counter　服務台／tourism bureau service center　觀光局旅客服務中心

Officers of the information counter can assist tourists to enjoy their trips.

服務台工作人員能協助旅客享有美好旅程。

◉insurance counter　保險櫃檯

There are several insurance counters at the airport for you to choose from.

在機場有幾個保險櫃檯供您選擇。

◉International Date Line (I.D.L)　國際換日線

We are crossing the International Date Line.

我們正飛越國際換日線。

◉international passenger 國際旅客

transit passenger 過境旅客

There are several free half day tours for international passengers/ transit passengers in Taipei.

台北有幾項免費的半天旅遊提供給國際旅客／過境旅客。

◉jet lag 飛機時差

Some people might feel disoriented due to jet lag.

一些人可能因為飛機時差，方位的判斷力降低。

memo

L

◉ landing 降落

We are now landing at Chiang Kai Shek International Airport.

我們現在在桃園中正國際機場降落。

◉ luggage scale 行李磅秤

Please put your luggage on the luggage scale. Thank you.

請將您的行李放在行李磅秤，謝謝！

◉ lavatory 洗手間

Could you tell me where the lavatory is? Thank you.

可以告訴我洗手間在哪嗎？謝謝！

◉ layover 外站過夜

We will have a layover in Paris.

我們會在巴黎過夜。

◉ life jacket (vest) 救生衣

Your individual life jacket is located in a pouch beneath your seat.

您的救生衣在您座椅下方。

◉ Lost and Found 失物招領

You may find your notebook at the Lost and Found.

您也許能在失物招領中心找到您的筆電。

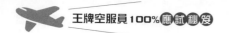
M

◉ **maintenance** 維修

Aircrafts require constant maintenance.

飛機需要經常保養維修。

◉ **medicine for airsickness** 暈機藥

Flight attendants cannot provide passengers with medicine for airsickness; make sure you have your own medicine when you are travelling.

空服員不能提供暈機藥給旅客，當你旅遊時記得攜帶自己的常備藥。

◉ **meal tray** 餐盤／**toothpick** 牙籤

You could find a toothpick in your meal tray.

您可以在餐盤上找到牙籤。

◉ **medical center** 醫療中心

If you feel sick or uncomfortable, you can always go to the medical center at the airport.

如果您覺得生病或不舒服，你可以去機場的醫療中心尋求協助。

◉ **metal detector** 金屬探測器

Please walk through the metal detector.

請通過金屬探測器。

● moving / automatic walkway 自動步道

When walking on an automatic walkway, please keep an eye on your children.

在自動步道上，請小心您的孩童。

① 應試前準備

② 應試技巧

③ 飛上青空情境大模擬

memo

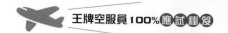

N

● non-endorsable 禁止轉讓

Some tickets are non-endorsable.

有些機票是禁止轉讓的。

● non-smoking Section (Area) 非吸煙區

This is a non-smoking section.

這是非吸煙區。

● non-stop flight 直飛班機

Is this a non-stop flight to Amsterdam?

這是直飛阿姆斯特丹的航班嗎？

O

◉ occupied 使用中／vacant 無人

The lavatory is vacant (occupied) now.

洗手間現在無人使用（有人使用）中。

◉ on time 準時

You must get to the boarding gate on time.

你必須準時到達登機門。

◉ one-way ticket 單程機票／round-trip ticket 來回機票

A one-way ticket is usually more expensive than a round–trip ticket. 單程機票通常比來回機票貴。

◉ vending machine 販賣機／out of order 故障

This vending machine is out of order.

這台販賣機故障了。

◉ overhead bin (compartment) 頭頂置物箱

Please put your baggage into the overhead bin. Thank you.

請將您的行李放置在頭頂置物箱，謝謝！

◉ oxygen mask 氧氣面罩

An oxygen mask will come down automatically from overhead in case of an emergency. 萬一當遇到緊急狀況時，氧氣面罩將會自動落下。

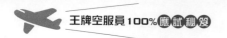

P

◉ **passenger** 旅客

The passengers boarded the plane at 11 a.m.

旅客們在上午 11 點登機。

◉ **passport** 護照

Keep an eye on your passport when you are travelling.

當你旅行時，一定要看好你的護照。

◉ **personal belongings** 個人物品

Please take your personal belongings with you.

請攜帶好您的個人物品。

◉ **processing** 處理中

The computer is processing flight data now. Wait a moment, please.

電腦現在正在處理飛航資訊，請稍後。

R

● reading light 閱讀燈

May I turn on the reading light for you?

我幫您打開閱讀燈吧？

● refueling stop 加油停留

This flight will make a refueling stop in Anchorage.

此航班會在安克拉治加油停留。

● reissue ticket 補發機票

I lost my air ticket accidentally Where can I reissue my ticket?

我不小心遺失了機票，請問我要去哪裡申請補發機票？

● rental counter 租車櫃檯／greeting area 到站等候區

You will find the rental counter in the greeting area.

在到站等候區，您會看到租車櫃檯。

● ramp (jetway/passenger bridge) 空橋

The passengers are using the ramp to board the airplane.

旅客們使用空橋登機。

● remote parking bay 接駁機坪

We will use a remote parking bay for this flight.

這個航班將使用接駁機坪。

◉ remote control / handset 遙控器

You can use the remote control to choose your movie channels.

您可以用遙控器選擇您的電影頻道。

◉ retractable landing gear 飛機起落架／fuel 油料／fuel tank 燃料箱

The fuel tank and retractable landing gear are important parts of the airplane.

燃料箱和飛機起落架是飛機重要的零件。

◉ runway 機場跑道／taxiing 滑行

The plane is taxiing along the runway.

飛機正在跑道上滑行。

S

◉ safety rules　安全規定

Before having a security check at the airport, please read the safety rules first.

在機場安全檢查前，請先詳讀安全規定。

◉ security check　安全檢查

Security check is important for flight safety.

安全檢查對飛航安全很重要。

◉ shuttle bus　接駁巴士／ taxi stand　計程車排班區

Where can I find your shuttle bus/ taxi stand at the airport?

請問你們的接駁車／計程車排班區在機場的什麼地方？

◉ seat back　椅背

Please upright your seat back when dining during the flight.

在機上用餐時，請豎直您的椅背。

◉ sightseeing　觀光

I am here for sightseeing. 我是來觀光的。

◉ slide　逃生用滑梯

In an emergency evacuation, make sure that you follow flight attendant's instructions carefully to prepare to jump on a slide.

在緊急逃生時，一定要遵照空服員的指示，跳上逃生用滑梯離開飛機。

◉ smoke hood 防煙面罩

We check smoke hoods and other equipment before the departure of every fight.

我們在每趟航班前會檢查防煙面罩與其它設備。

◉ smoking room 吸煙室

Many airports have smoking rooms for smokers.

許多機場設有吸煙室。

◉ stand-by ticket counter 補票櫃檯

I am afraid that your ticket has expired. You need to go to a stand-by ticket counter to get a new one.

您的機票過期了，您必須去補票櫃檯買一張新的。

◉ survival kit 救生箱

There is a survival kit in the aircraft.

飛機上有救生箱。

◉ safety demonstration 安全示範

Flight attendants are about to show the safety demonstration shortly.

空服員馬上將為您做安全示範。

T

● tailwind 順風

We might arrive at New York early as we are now flying with a tailwind.

我們現在順風，可能提早抵達紐約。

● time zone 時區

Which time zone is your city located in?

請問你的城市位於哪個時區？

● trolley (luggage cart) 行李推車

Excuse me, where can I find a trolley?

請問哪裡有行李推車？

● timetable 時刻表

The timetable at the airport might be subject to change sometimes. Don't forget to keep an eye on it.

機場的時刻表有時會變動，別忘了注意。

● Terminal 1 (2) 第一（二）航站

I am afraid that you are in the wrong terminal. Your flight should be in Terminal one.

我想你到錯航站囉！你的航班是在第一航站。

◉ turbulence 亂流

We might experience some turbulence during the flight. For your safety, please fasten your seat belt all the time.

航程中我們可能會經過一些不穩定氣流，為了您的安全，請隨時繫上安全帶。

◉ toilet with handrail 設有扶手的洗手間

On your right side, you can find the toilet with handrail.

在妳的右手邊，你會看到設有扶手的洗手間。

◉ tourist visa 觀光簽證

You need to apply for a tourist visa if you want to travel to Bangkok.

如果你想去曼谷觀光，你需要申請觀光簽證。

◉ turnaround 當天來回

To us, Hong Kong is a turnaround flight.

香港對我們而言，是當天來回航班。

◉ transfer correspondence 轉機櫃檯

You might go to the transfer correspondence directly when we arrive at the airport.

當我們抵達機場，您需要直接去轉機櫃檯。

◉ transit lounge　過境大廳

Transit passengers can take some rest in the transit lounge.

過境旅客可以在過境大廳休息。

◉ travelling information　旅遊資訊

You can get great travelling information from the information center. 您可以在服務台獲得很棒的旅遊資訊。

◉ touch screen　觸控螢幕

This is a touch screen. You can just use your fingertips to control your in-flight entertainment system.

這是觸控螢幕，您只需要用指尖就能控制您的機上娛樂系統。

◉ tray table　餐桌

Please put down your tray table for dining.

請將餐桌放下準備用餐。

◉ trolley case　行李箱（有滾輪的）

A good trolley case will avoid travel hassles.

一個好的行李箱能避免旅途困擾。

◉ trolley　餐車

We have to make sure all trolleys are well locked when the flight is about to land.

飛機降落前，我們必須要確認所有餐車都鎖好。

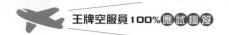

U・V

◉ unaccompanied baggage 託運行李

Your unaccompanied baggage has cleared customs.

你的託運行李已經通過海關檢查。

◉ unaccompanied minor declaration form 無監護人隨行申請表格／
unaccompanied passenger (child passenger) 無人陪同孩童

Children between 7 and 12 year who travel alone are classified as unaccompanied passengers. Their parents or guardians are required to fill and sign unaccompanied minor declaration forms at the check-in counters.

七歲至十二歲單獨旅行的孩童歸類為無人陪同孩童遊客。他們的父母或監護人必須在報到櫃檯填寫無監護人隨行表格，同時簽名。

◉ VIP lounge 貴賓室

You can get free drinks and desserts in our VIP lounges.

我們貴賓室提供免費飲料與甜點。

W

◉ waste bin (dustbin) 垃圾桶

Throw your empty bottles into the waste bin before you go to security check at the airport.

在機場安全檢查前，將您身上空瓶丟進垃圾桶。

◉ weight limit 重量限制

Your luggage exceeds weight limit. You might consider re-arranging your luggage or paying extra fee.

您的行李超過重量限制，您可能要考慮重新整理行李或支付額外費用。

◉ wheelchair 輪椅

Our ground staff has prepared a wheelchair for you and will accompany you at the airport.

我們的地勤人員已經替您準備好輪椅，同時會在機場陪同您。

◉ Wireless Internet Access (Wi-Fi) 無線上網

Our airport offers passengers high-speed Wireless Internet Access.

我們的機場提供旅客高速無線上網。

◉ window shade 機上遮陽窗板／take off 起飛

Please pull up the window shade when the flight is taking off.

起飛時請將窗板打開。

① 應試前準備

② 應試技巧

③ 飛上青空情境大模擬

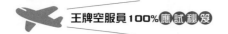
◉waiting room 候機室

The waiting room at the airport is spacious.

機場的候機室很寬敞。

memo

航空相關重要句型

This is the pre-boarding announcement for flight 111 to New York.

這是 111 班機飛往紐約的登機廣播。

Excuse me, may I see your boarding pass?

不好意思，可以看一下您的登機證嗎？

Do you have your passport with you?

您的護照在您身上嗎？

Welcome aboard.

歡迎登機。

I am afraid that your bag exceeds the size restrictions.

我擔心您的袋子超過尺寸限制了。

My seat cannot recline.

我的座椅無法往後倒。

My earphones don't seem to be working.

我的耳機好像不能使用。

How long does it take to get to Bangkok?

請問飛到曼谷需要多久時間？

1 應試前準備

2 應試技巧

3 飛上青空情境大模擬

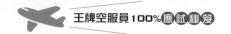

Is it possible to get an aisle seat?

請問我能換到走道的位置嗎？

I have requested a vegetarian meal. Could you help me to confirm it?

我訂了素食餐，可以請你幫忙確認嗎？

Could I use my laptop on board?

我可以在機上使用筆記型電腦嗎？

Is the flight on time?

這班飛機會準時嗎？

Please fasten your seat belt and put your seat up.

請繫安全帶，將您的椅背豎起。

For your safety, the use of personal electronic devices is prohibited during take-off and landing.

為了您的安全，在飛機起飛與降落時，請勿使用個人電子用品。

You may unfasten your seat belt.

您現在可以將安全帶解開。

We will be arriving at XX Airport in twenty minutes.

在 20 分鐘，我們將抵達 XX 機場。

We are going to take off. Would you please switch your electronic devices off?

我們即將起飛，請收起您的個人電子用品。

The cabin door will be closed once all the passengers are seated.

在所有旅客就座後，客艙門將關閉。

This is a non-smoking flight. All the lavatories are equipped with smoke detectors.

這是禁煙班機，所有洗手間都裝有煙霧偵測器。

Please put your bag under the seat in front of you or in the overhead bins.

請將您的行李放置於座位下方或上方的行李櫃上。

Would you care for a blanket/ an immigration form/ a drink?

您需要毛毯／入境表格／飲料嗎？

Please pay attention to the following safety demonstration.

請留意以下安全示範。

Would you care for something to drink?

請問您想喝些什麼飲料？

We are serving meals in 30 minutes.

我們會在 30 分鐘左右供應餐點。

If you need any assistance, please contact any of our crew members.

若您需要任何協助，請與我們任何一位空服組員聯繫。

Wish you have a pleasant journey.

祝您有個愉快的旅程。

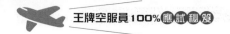

Is anything I can do for you?

有什麼我能為您做的嗎？

Which currency do you prefer?

請問您想使用何種幣值？

Do you prefer to pay with cash or by card?

請問您想使用現金或信用卡？

Here is your meal. Enjoy it.

這是您的餐點，請享用。

May I have some more bread, please?

可以再給我一些麵包嗎？

Do you have any instant noodles?

請問有泡麵嗎？

May I take your tray away?

我可以幫您收走餐盤嗎？

Please return your seat immediately.

請立刻回到您的座位。

Please put your seatback upright and stow your tray table.
請豎直椅背，收好餐桌。

I am afraid that I will miss my connecting flight.
我擔心我會錯過我的轉接班機。

memo

面試題庫整理

❶ 30 秒中英文答題技巧

答題技巧

　　永遠站在招募公司方思考，陳述自己能對公司有何貢獻？例如：良好的應變能力、優異的外語能力、高 EQ、細心、關懷他人的特質、有責任感、團隊合作精神、口條佳、待人親切、充滿愛心、體諒他人、重視安全、從不遲到、自我要求高……等等。

忌答內容

　　以自己的利益為出發點。例如：喜歡旅遊、想環遊世界、趁年輕想到處體驗異文化、從小夢想成為一名空服員、增加人生閱歷……等等。

基本英文句型 12 種時態

　　雖然文法書上寫了很多使用各種時態的時機，但以我的經驗，大部分的時態用常理理解就可學會，無需死背。先選擇四種狀態（簡單式、完成式、進行式、完成進行式）中的其中一種，再選擇時間（過去、現在、未來），就能輕鬆答題。例如：我有一本書。你會選擇哪種狀態？「簡單式」。那你會選擇哪種時間？「現在式」。所以答案是現在簡單式：I have a book.非常容易吧？現在讓我們把 12 種時態句型記起來，然後用理解的方式多加練習即可。

用12種時態的表達方式如下：

簡單式

現在簡單式：主詞＋現在式動詞

I write a letter every day.

我每天寫信。

現在簡單式：主詞＋過去式動詞

I wrote a letter yesterday.

我昨天寫了一封信。

未來簡單式：主詞＋will＋原形動詞

I will write a letter tomorrow.

我明天會寫信。

完成式

現在完成式：主詞＋have＋過去分詞

I have written the letter.

我已經寫好信了。

過去完成式：主詞＋had＋過去分詞

I had written the letter when my mother came.

我媽媽來的時候，我正好寫好信。

未來完成式：主詞＋will have＋過去分詞

I will have written the letter before my mother comes.

等我媽媽來的時候，我就會寫好信了。

進行式

現在進行式：主詞＋is/am/are＋現在分詞

I am writing a letter now.

我現在正在寫信。

過去進行式：主詞＋was/were＋現在分詞

I was writing a letter when my mother came.

我母親來的時候，我正在寫信。

未來進行式：主詞＋will be＋現在分詞

I will be writing a letter when my mother comes.

我母親來的時候，我會在寫信。

完成進行式

現在完成進行式：主詞＋has/ have been＋現在分詞

I have been writing a letter for one hour.

我寫信寫了一個小時了。

過去完成進行式：主詞＋had been＋現在分詞

I had been writing a letter for three hours when my mother called.

我母親打電話來的時候，我已經寫信寫了三個小時了。

未來完成進行式：主詞＋will have been＋現在分詞
I will have been learning English for ten years by the beginning of next year.
到明年初為止，我已經學英文學了十年了。

memo

面試題庫整理
❷ 簡易生活問題、描述個人經驗

簡易生活問題

實用英文句型

◉ 謝謝你的關心。

   例 Thanks for asking.

   Thanks for your concern.

◉ 除了……

   Apart from / Except（除……外，不包括在內）

   Apart from/ Besides / In addition to（除……外，還有……）

   例 除了小籠包外，台灣還有很多著名的小吃。

   Apart from Xiaolongbao, there are many famous street food in Taiwan.

Q1
Track 07

Have you had breakfast this morning? What did you have?

今天早上有吃早餐嗎？ 吃了什麼？

A1 Thanks for asking. I have fried eggs and milk. Breakfast is the most important meal in a day. I always think it's necessary to have breakfast every day, particularly today. Today is very important for me. I need energy and clear thoughts to prove that I can be a great flight attendant in your team.

　　謝謝您的關懷。今天早上吃了荷包蛋和牛奶。早餐是一日最重要的一餐，我認為每天都需要吃早餐，尤其在我人生中非常重要的今天；我需要滿滿的能量與清晰的思緒，證明自己能成為貴公司優秀的空服員。

描述個人經驗

實用英文句型

◉ Among various kinds of…, 在各種……之中

Among various kinds of sports, I like dancing in particular.

在各種運動中，我最喜歡跳舞。

◉ enjoy / finish / keep / practice 後接動名詞（V-ing），而非不定詞（to V）

I enjoy learning English. 我喜歡學習英語。

I finish doing my homework. 我完成我的作業。

I keep exercising every day. 我每天做運動。

I practice dancing every day. 我每天練習跳舞。

Q2
Track 08

What do you do in your free time?
在空閒時間做些什麼活動？

A2 I enjoy doing a variety of activities, such as surfing, listening to music, dancing and reading. Listening to music is my favorite. I like to know different cultures through music. Whenever I went to other countries, I always took CDs with me as souvenirs. I have CDs from Thailand, France, Japan, and Hong Kong. Even though I cannot understand the lyrics, I can still feel the beauty of music and those music always make me recall my happy travelling memories. If I have an opportunity to become a flight attendant, I will keep collecting CDs from different countries and sharing them with other people.

我喜歡各種不同的活動，像衝浪、聽音樂、跳舞和閱讀。特別是聽音樂，這是我最喜歡做的一件事。我喜歡透過聽音樂了解不同文化。當我去其它國家，我總是會買 CD 當紀念品。我目前有從泰國、法國、日本和香港帶回來的 CD。雖然聽不懂歌的內容，但仍能感受到音樂的美妙，同時喚起旅行的快樂記憶。如果我有機會能成為貴公司的空服員，我會繼續收集來自不同國家的音樂，同時跟大家分享。

Q3
Track 09

Have you ever lied?
你曾經說過謊嗎？

A3 Yes. I have lied, although I expect myself to be the honest person. In some situations, lies, not truth, can comfort people. I heard the story about two patients in a hospice. The patient who got the window bed comforted another patient by telling him how wonderful the scenery outside it is every day. One day, he passed away and another patient moved to the window bed. He found nothing but cold cement walls outside the window.

My sister had ever lived in a hospital for a while. I told her that she looks great every day and might go home tomorrow. I admitted that's a lie. However, that lie motivated my sister and she has a wonderful and healthy life now. Telling lie is not always wrong; it depends on how you tell them.

是的，我說過謊。雖然我自許成為誠實的人，但有些情況，謊言會比真話能撫慰人心。我聽過一個醫院的故事，有兩位住在安寧病房的病人，

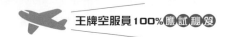
靠窗床位的病人總是跟另外一位病人述說外面景色的美好，安撫他的情緒。當有一天靠窗床位病人離開人世，另外一位病人換到靠窗的床位時，他發現窗外只看得到對面的水泥牆，什麼景色也沒有。

我的姊姊曾經住過一段時間的醫院，我每天都跟她說她的氣色很好，明天就能回家了。我承認那是謊話，但也因為這樣的謊言激勵了姊姊，讓她現在能健康的生活。我覺得說謊並不是一定錯的，但看說的人的怎麼說。

Q4
Track 10

What was your favorite subject in school？
你在校最喜愛的科目是什麼？

A4 My favorite subject is Mandarin. Chinese culture is profound and has deeply impressed me, whether it is expressed through beautiful poems or meaningful articles. I hope I can share Chinese culture with other people. Actually, this is one of the reasons I want to be a flight attendant. I think flight attendants have more opportunities to communicate with people. I wish people can like Chinese culture as I do.

我在學校最喜歡的科目是中文。中華文化博大精深，無論是優美的詩詞歌賦或是饒富意義的文章，都讓我感受深刻。我希望能將中華文化分享給更多人，這也是讓我想成為空服員的其中一個原因。空服員的工作能讓我有更多機會接觸更多的人，我想讓更多人能和我一樣，感受到中文的美好。

Q5
Track 11
How do you maintain your weight? What kind of exercise do you like the most?
你如何維持體重？你喜歡什麼運動？

A5 I keep having a healthy life by living a life of moderation. I have 3 meals every day and eat healthily. The benefit of a healthy life is that I don't need to maintain my weight on purpose. I like Salsa, which is my favorite exercise. Salsa dance can release stress, help myself get concentrated and keep my body's ability to balance improved I highly recommend everybody can try it.

　　我生活有節制，以維持健康的生活。每天正常吃三餐，同時吃得很健康。維持健康生活的好處就是不需要刻意維持體重。我喜歡跳 Salsa，Salsa 是我最喜歡的運動，Salsa 能釋放壓力、集中心智、訓練身體平衡，建議大家都能嘗試看看。

1 應試前準備

2 應試技巧

3 飛上青空情境大模擬

面試題庫整理

❸ 對事情的看法

對事情的看法

實用英文句型

- 我相信 I believe that...

- 我深信 I am greatly convinced (that)

- 我覺得 I think that...

- 我的意見是 In my opinion,...

- 以我的經驗 In my experience,...

- 我想説的是 I'd like to say...

- 就我而言 From my perspective,...

- 就我而言 As far as I'm concerned,...

- 如果您問我 If you ask me,...

Q1
Track 12

What's the differences between confidence and arrogance?
請問自信與自負的差別？

A1 In my opinion, the difference between confidence and arrogance is that confident people tend to listen to and accept others' suggestions, while arrogant people don't. People with confidence express their own ideas, but at the same time, they also communicate with others and adjust their own thinking. However, arrogant ones will insist their own opinions and not accept others' advice. This is my personal opinion about this question.

就我而言，自信和自負的差別在於自信的人傾向聆聽並接受他人的意見，但自負的人則不是如此。自信的人會表達自己的想法，但也同時會與其他人溝通自己的想法。若旁人有別的想法，自信的人會思考調整。而自負的人表達自己的想法後，若旁人有別的想法，自負的人還是會堅持己見。這是我對自信與自負的想法。

Q2
Track 13

Do you consider yourself a success?
你覺得自己成功嗎？

A2 Every individual has a different definition of success. I consider myself a success at this stage as I am facing everything in my life positively. I pursue my goal with faiths and put efforts into it. This is

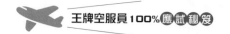
my definition of success.

　　每個人對成功的定義不同，我覺得自己每天積極認真地生活，並帶著信念，努力追求自己的目標，在現階段，我覺得自己是成功的。

 Q3 Track 14　What kinds of decisions are most difficult for you?
什麼樣的決定對你而言是困難的？

A3 In my point of view, all things are easy if they are done willingly. If they are things I can do, no matter how hard they are, I believe I can conquer them all and making decisions in such situations is never difficult to me. However, there are lots of things people cannot conquer in the world, such as life and death. Whenever this moment comes, making decisions becomes a tough task to me. It's particularly hard to let go when facing death.

　　我覺得天下無難事，只怕有心人。只要是我能努力達成的事，不管事情困難與否，事在人為，我相信我都能一一克服；在這樣的情況下做決定，對我來說也不困難。但世界上還是有很多事情，是人怎麼努力也無法克服的，像是生老病死。對我來說，這時做決定對我而言就是困難的，而最大的課題就是學習釋懷。

Q4 Track 15

What kind of contributions will you make to our airline?
你覺得你能為我們航空公司帶來什麼貢獻？

A4 A flight attendant is the ambassador of airline. Most of the time, people judge the performance of airline by the impressions flight attendants gave them. Therefore, I think the best contribution I can make to the airline is being a great ambassador of airline. I know that it is not easy to reach this goal, but I will try my best to follow company's visions and hope I can be the best spokesperson of your company.

空服員是航空公司的品牌大使，航空公司在人們心中的評價，有很多是來自於對空服員的觀感與表現。我能對航空公司做的最好貢獻就是成為一位稱職的空服員，成為航空公司最佳的品牌大使。當然，要成為最佳的品牌大使非常不容易，但我會努力朝著公司的目標前進，希望能成為最佳的航空公司代言人。

Q5 Track 16

How important is appearance?
你覺得外表如何重要？

A5 I think appearance is very important. Most people will be attracted by beautiful things, such as fine scenery and mouth-watering food. That is the human nature. However, for the human beings, appearance doesn't equal a great body figure; what truly matters is the beauty inside. Some beauties look beautiful but hard to get along with. Girls next door might not be your love at first sight; however, you would like to spend more time with them. Therefore, in my opinion, I do think people have to take a good care of appearance; however, don't overweigh the outer beauty too much. Keeping the outer appearance clean and tidy is fine, but taking too much time keeping it perfect is not necessary.

　　我覺得外表非常重要，因為大多數的人都會被漂亮的東西吸引，就像漂亮的風景、賣相好的食物。這是人的本性，人之常情。但外表不單指先天的身材，真正重要的是內在美。就像冰山美人雖然讓人覺得賞心悅目，卻不易親近；而具有鄰家女孩氣質的女生，雖不是最出眾的，但就是讓人覺得很想多跟她在一起。我覺得人要注重外表，但不要過度追求。維持外表的乾淨整齊很好，但過度的追求外表的完美，對我而言就不是必須的。

Q6
Track 17

How does Facebook affect our life?
Facebook 如何影響我們的生活？

A6 In my opinion, Facebook totally changes our life. Since we have Facebook, we cannot enjoy meals without taking photos. After taking photos, some people will upload photos immediately instead of enjoying great meals. People value taking photos more than spending time with friends. We might have hundreds of friends on Facebook, but we hardly know most of them. I mean we might just meet them once or twice in person. This is how Facebook affects our life.

　　就我而言，Facebook 完全改變了我們的生活。我感受最深的是，自從有了 Facebook 之後，大家在餐點送來時，不再是趁熱吃，而是要先拍照上傳 Facebook 才能吃。自拍的時間變多了，跟朋友外出時交談的時間變少了。Facebook 上朋友可能有上百人，但大部份幾乎都不認識，然後真正碰面也不過一兩次吧。Facebook 正是這樣地影響了我們的生活。

Q7 **What's your dream?**
你的夢想是什麼？

Track 18

A7 My dream is helping people to have a better life. Evaluating my personality and ability, I find being a flight attendant can help me fulfill my dream. I would like to take care of passengers who take flights and travel with different purposes, understand every passenger's needs, soothe passengers' emotions, and handle a variety of situations. For me, being a flight attendant is very challenging and I have confidence that I can do it well.

　　我的夢想是能盡一己之力幫助別人。評量自己的性格和能力後，發現空服員是最能達成我夢想的職業。我想要在高空中照顧因不同目的飛行和旅遊的乘客、了解旅客的需求、安撫旅客的情緒，並處理各種突發狀況。對我而言，空服員是一份非常具挑戰性的工作，我有信心能做得很好。

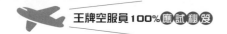
Q8 Track 19

What's your favorite city?
你最喜歡哪一個城市？

A8 I like every city in the world as every city has its own characteristics. If I really have to choose one city, I will choose the city I live in -Taipei. It's the place I grew up since I was very young. Every corner of my neighborhood, including the breakfast shop and the aunt next door, brought me the greatest memories about here. The deep emotional connection between Taipei and I is my precious treasure. I want to travel to different cities and bring the advantages of those cities to Taipei, my favorite city.

我喜歡世界上所有城市，每個城市都有自己的特色。但要選出最喜歡的城市，那就是我一直居住的城市-台北。因為從小生活在這個城市，在這裡有從小到大住家生活的美好回憶，像是常吃的早餐店、隔壁的鄰居阿姨；我對這個城市有特別的感情，這份感情也是我最珍貴的寶物。我想到世界不同的城市旅行，將不同城市的優點帶回台北，這個我最喜歡的城市。

Q9 Track 20

How to become your best friend?
當你的好朋友需要具備什麼條件？

A9 To be my best friend is very simple: just to be sincere, nothing more. I believe sincerity is the greatest gift people can give. Sincere person can bring happiness and warmth to people. I've been asking myself to be a sincere person and to make friends with sincere friends. People might have different growing backgrounds, different thoughts and different life styles; however, I believe that everything will be fine if we communicate with each other in a sincere attitude.

當我的好朋友只要真誠就好，不需要具備其它條件。真誠是一個人能給另外一個人最好的禮物。真誠的人能帶給人們幸福和溫暖。我一直要求自己成為一個真誠的人，也想要和真誠的人交往，雖然每個人有不同的生長背景、不同的想法和不同的生活方式，但只要能用真誠的態度溝通，相信一切都會很好。

Q10
Track 21

What's your dream job?
你心中夢想的職業是什麼？

A10 My dream job is being a flight attendant and I believe I am good at it. I always want to dedicate myself to helping people. After evaluating my personality and ability, I found being a flight attendant is the best way for me to fulfill my dream. I can take a good care of passengers who take flights and travel with different purposes. In order to become a great flight attendant, I always train myself to handle emergencies by being equipped with possible solutions to various situations in advance. You won't regret to have me in your team.

我夢想的職業是空服員，而且我相信自己能做得很好。一直以來，我希望能盡一己之力幫助別人。在評估自己的個性和能力後，我發現空服員是最能實現我夢想的工作。我相信我能照顧為了不同目的搭乘飛機和旅遊的乘客。為了能成為一位好的空服員，我總是讓自己事先準備好應付各種情況的解決方案，來訓練自己處理突發狀況的能力。選擇我成為您團隊的一員，相信您不會後悔的。

 Q11 Track 22 **Where do you prefer to live, in a big city or the country? And why?**
你喜歡住在城市還是鄉村？ 為什麼？

A11 I prefer to live in a big city as I like to meet different people. I enjoy talking with people and sharing experiences with them.Every person has his or her own different story, and I always can learn from them. There are 194 nations in the world. I hope I will have an opportunity to meet people from all over the world.

我喜歡住在城市，因為我喜歡與不同人接觸。我喜歡跟人交談並分享彼此生活經驗。每個人有不同的故事，我總能從別人的故事中學習。世界上有 194 個國家，我希望能有機會接觸更多來自世界不同角落的人。

 Q12 Track 23 **Do you like to be a leader or a follower?**
你喜歡當領導者還是跟隨者？

A12 I will say it depends. If it's something I am good at it or other people in the group might not have experiences in that area, I will be happy to be a leader. However, if it's something I am not familiar with and other people have more experiences in it, I will be happy to be a follower.

對於這個問題，我的答案是看情況。如果當時團隊中沒有人比我有經驗處理，我會樂於當領導者。但如果有其它人更有經驗處理，我會樂於當跟隨者。

Q13
Track 24

What motivates you？
什麼因素能激勵你？

A13 My motivation for the life is having hopes. My motto is "Tomorrow is another day." Therefore, no matter what happened today, I will always have hope for tomorrow. Having hope is a good thing. I think when people are kind and sincere, always have hopes for tomorrow, all good things will happen in their life.

激勵我積極樂觀過每一天的因素是希望。我的人生座右銘是：「明天又是嶄新的一天。」，所以不管今天發生什麼事情，我都會對明天懷抱著希望。擁有希望是好事，我覺得人只要善良、真誠，永遠對明天懷抱希望，所有的好事都會降臨在他身上。

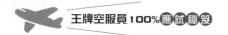

Q14

Track 25

How do you handle criticism？
你如何面對批評？

A14 Most people have to handle criticism in life. Whenever I need to face criticism, I will review myself first since it might be caused by my improper behaviors. If I do something wrong, I will apologize immediately and seek for solutions. If I cannot do anything about the criticism, I will face it, try to stay peaceful and keep the life going on in the way as usual.

　　人生在世，我想大多數的人都需要處理批評這件事。遇到批評時，我會先檢討自己的言行舉止是否失當，若是因為我自身緣故造成，我會馬上道歉並尋求解決方法。若是批評導因於其它外在，我無法控制的因素，我會以平常心面對批評。

Q15

Track 26

Are you willing to learn a foreign language？
你願意學習外國語言嗎？

A15 I enjoy learning new things, especially languages. I think languages are the great communication tool. It's no doubt that giving smiles and using body languages are great ways as well; however, if we want to know more about different people, countries, and cultures, languages will play a key role. If foreigners know you are try to learn their languages, they will feel grateful even though you cannot speak it well. Try to imagine the feeling when you hear foreigners say thank you to you in Chinese. Won't you feel grateful? Therefore, I am more than happy to learn foreign languages.

　　我非常喜歡學習新的事物，尤其是語言，因為我認為語言是人與人互相溝通了解的媒介。雖然笑容與肢體語言也是不可或缺的溝通管道，但如果想深入了解一個人、一個國家、甚或是一種文化，語言就扮演了非常重要的角色。若是外國人知道你很努力地學習他們的語言，想了解他們的文化，即使你說得不是很好，他們也會很開心，同時肯定你對他們的用心。就像我們聽到外國人用中文跟我們說謝謝那樣，你不會覺得很開心嗎？所以我非常願意學習任何一種新的語言。

面試題庫整理

❹ 臨場反應問題

答題重點

　　在準備這類題型時，一定要記得這類題型雖沒有範圍，但有規則的。在準備答案與臨場應答時，心中想著空服員的特質和工作內容，無論是什麼問題，例如題庫中問的水果或花之類的，答案都要與空服員的特質和工作內容有關，這是最重要的規則與重點，一定要牢記在心。

Q1
Track 27

Please recommend one fruit to the examiners.
推薦考官吃一種水果。

A1 I will recommend kiwi fruit to you because I really like to share my own experiences with people. I eat kiwi fruit everyday and really think it is a great fruit. Kiwi fruit is rich in vitamin c, dietary fiber and nutrition. What's more, kiwi fruit is good for flight attendants because it keeps our digestive system function properly. Flight attendants might not have regular living styles and couldn't have meals on time when they are on duty, so their digestive system might need extra cares. Therefore, I think kiwi fruit will be a great fruit for you.

　　我會推薦我自己常吃的水果——奇異果。因為我是一個很喜歡分享的人，我每天都會吃奇異果，我真心覺得奇異果是很棒的水果。有豐富的維

生素 C、膳食纖維，營養成份高。尤其奇異果能幫助消化，我覺得非常適合空服工作的人食用。因為擔任空服工作，有時用餐時間短且無法固定，生活作息也無法很規律，我想奇異果是非常適合考官的水果。

Q2

Track 28

Which flower do you think can represent me?
請用一種花來形容考官。

A2 I will say dandelion. Dandelion is a flower which can survive anywhere. When its seed becomes mature, it will go with the wind to the new place and breed new flowers. To me, you, as an examiner in the airline company, you must have perseverance and can survive everywhere. I wish I can be like you, like dandelion.

　　我會用蒲公英來形容您。蒲公英是一種生存力極強的植物，種子成熟後，會隨風飄曳到新的地方，孕育新的花朵。對我而言，能在航空公司擔任考官的您，一定具備像蒲公英一樣堅忍的個性，無論在什麼地方都能生存。我也希望自己能像您一樣，成為像蒲公英一樣的人。

Q3

Track 29

If you only have 5 decks of cards for a 6 people group, what will you do?
如果 6 人一團，但你只有 5 副撲克牌，請問你會怎麼處理？

A3 I will not tell passengers how many cards I have. I will ask them to divide into 3 groups and then every group can get a deck of cards. They might say they all want to have an individual one for a souvenir.

Then I will tell them: it is such a pity if you don't play cards now. Card games can give you happy memories if you play during the flight. If you don't open it and keep it at home, it will be just a deck of cards. Each deck of cards of ours is made to give you a great time during the flight. Besides, I would tell those passengers they still could have another deck of cards in their returned flights, right? I believe most people will gladly accept it if we use humor to create great travelling memories for them. If they still insist that they want to have their own deck of cards, I will distribute 5 decks of cards and for the one who doesn't have the deck of cards, I'll ask him/ her to leave the address so that I could send the deck of cards to him/ her. Like playing chess, there won't be only one solution to dealing with things, we have to come out up with the best solutions when facing different circumstances. I am confident in my problem-solving ability and qualified for being a flight attendant.

　　我不會跟旅客說我有多少撲克牌，而是請他們分成 3 組，每組分得一副撲克牌。他們可能會說我們每個人都要帶回去做紀念，所以每個人都要自己的一副。這時我會跟他們說，撲克牌如果不打開玩，只是帶回去做紀念太可惜了。我們撲克牌可以給你們更好的紀念，就是現在打開玩，擁有一起玩的記憶才珍貴。若是他們還堅持要一個人一副，我會跟他們說，你們還有回程班機啊！我相信用幽默的方式幫他們創造旅行的記憶，大部分的人都能開心接受的。若他們還是非常堅持，最後的方式就是請一個人留地址，我會寄送撲克牌給他。我覺得對於事情解決的方式絕不是只有一種，就像下棋一樣，要能依不同的狀況，想出最好的方法。我對自己解決問題的能力有信心，相信自己能勝任空服工作。

Q4
Track 30

Recommend one interest that can keep flight attendants away from feeling alone.
推薦可以排遣空服員寂寞的興趣。

A4 I will recommend origami. I personally enjoy making origami works so much as I think origami is an interest that can be shared. I often give out my origami works to other people, and they all are happy to receive them. I think origami is an activity you can do anytime, which is very suitable for flight attendants. When flight attendants stay in the hotels in other cities, origami works can be room decoration materials. And when flight attendants need to move to another city, they can give their origami works to passengers. I think passengers will be glad to receive them. Moreover, when I am making origami works, I always think I can share these with people, and I do not feel lonely at all. Those are reasons why I would like to recommend origami to you.

　　我會推薦摺紙。我個人非常喜愛摺紙，因為摺紙是個能分享的興趣。我常常折紙鶴、星星送給身邊的人，他們都很開心能收到我的摺紙。而且摺紙不需要特別場地，隨時隨地都能摺，我想應該非常適合空服員的生活型態和工作。在外地飯店時，自己摺的紙可以布置房間。要換下一個地點時，可以把摺紙作品送給機上旅客，相信旅客也會很開心的。而且在摺紙時，你會想著能和人分享這些作品，一點都不會覺得寂寞。所以我想把這項興趣推薦給大家。

應試前準備 ❶

應試技巧 ❷

飛上青空情境大模擬 ❸

面試題庫整理

chapter 5

❺ **關於台灣**

答題重點

　　在應試前，建議以台灣推廣者或是以台灣旅行者的心態了解台灣，無論是台灣景點、文化、交通、當紅的旅遊方式、知名餐廳、著名小吃。由於範圍很廣，資訊很多，所以建議大家在各個分類上，選擇自己有興趣的深入研究，並在答題時強調自己是個喜歡分享的人，分享自己喜愛的事總是會更吸引人。

實用英文句型

◉ 我建議……

例 我建議你更新你的履歷。

I recommend / suggest/propose that you update your resume.

I recommend / suggest/propose your updating your resume

I recommend / suggest/propose that you update your resume

I recommend / suggest/propose you update your resume

◉ 在此介紹的是在這個答題分類中，會常使用到的 if 句型

如果我是……

例 如果我是旅客的導遊，我會建議他參觀故宮博物院。

If I am a tour guide for the passage, I will recommend him visiting the National Palace Museum.

◉ 注意重點

　　If 條件句中，if 後面的動詞絕對不會用到 will 這個未來式動詞。

Q1
Track 31

Recommend a Taipei one-day tour (including meals) to a couple on a flight.

推薦機上情侶台北一日遊（包括餐點）。

A1 If I don't take their previous travel experiences to Taipei and their preferences into consideration, I will share my favorite MRT one day tour. First of all, I will recommend MRT Donmen Station. They can enjoy the atmosphere of Yongkang street, and go to taste the food at the Michelin One-Star restaurant–Din Tai Fung. I personally recommend Pork XiaoLong Bao, House Steamed Chicken Soup, Shrimp Fried Rice and Mini Red Bean Buns. Then they can go to MRT Danshui station to eat famous Oily Bean Curd (Ah Gei), visit Fort Santo Domingo, take a boat to Bali to ride bicycles, and drop by the Shihsanghang Museum of Archaeology. When the night comes, they can go to MRT Xinbeitou station, choosing one of hot spring hotels to enjoy dinner and hot spring to end their day.

　　如果在不考慮這對情侶是第幾次到台北，有沒有特別偏好之類的，我會分享我自己喜愛的捷運一日遊。首先是捷運東門站的永康街，永康街除了世界知名的米其林一星鼎泰豐本店外，附近店家氛圍也是外國人很喜愛的。到了鼎泰豐，除了小籠包之外，蝦仁蛋炒飯、雞湯和迷你豆沙包也是不能錯過的。之後到淡水捷運站逛淡水老街，去紅毛城、吃阿給，然後搭船到八里騎自行車，順道去十三行博物館。晚上到新北投捷運站的溫泉飯店吃溫泉晚餐，泡溫泉，結束美好的一天。

1 應試前準備

2 應試技巧

3 飛上青空情境大模擬

Q2 How will you introduce Taiwanese foods to foreigners？

Track 32　你會怎麼跟外國朋友介紹台灣小吃？

A2 Taiwanese foods are famous and even CNN has selected top 40 Taiwanese foods. My foreign friends always have their favorite foods to eat up. The style of Taiwanese food is a combination of the cuisine of the Min Nan, Chaojou and FuJian Chinese communities, along with Japanese cooking. If I am the tour guide to introduce Taiwanese foods to foreigners, I will ask them their preference. For instance, if they like beef, I will introduce them beef noodle and braised pork rice . If they like seafood, oyster omelet and milkfish will be on my list. After meals, traditional desserts such as bubble tea and shaved ice mountain will be recommended to have without doubt. I believe those foods will bring foreign friends wonderful memories about Taiwan.

　　台灣小吃世界知名，連 CNN 都曾選出 40 種必吃台灣小吃。我的外國朋友來台灣前，總是已經選出他們心中的最愛。台灣小吃融合了閩南、潮州、客家與中國食的文化，同時也有日本烹調的方式在內。如果讓我介紹台灣小吃給國外朋友，因為台灣小吃種類繁多，我會先詢問他們喜歡吃肉類還是海鮮？若喜歡吃肉類，我會介紹牛肉麵和魯肉飯。若喜歡吃海鮮，那蚵仔煎和虱目魚就會是我介紹重點。用完餐後，甜點當然不可少。珍珠奶茶和刨冰也是一定要享用的。我相信上述的食物一定能為國外朋友留下對台灣的美好回憶。

Q3
Track 33

Which tourist attractions in Taiwan will you recommend to foreign travelers?

你會推薦哪個台灣景點給外國旅客？

A3 Taiwan is a country with the most diverse geographical and cultural features in Asia. People in Taiwan have gorgeous beaches, hot springs, night markets, and etc. Travelers always can find interesting places to go to. If I have a chance to give them a tour to visit Taiwan, I will find out what they want to do first. After all, there are many places to go with limited time. If they like beaches, Kenting will be a great place for them. The warm tropical weather makes Kenting a favorite travelling destination in winter. Surfing and scuba diving are popular activities there. If they like temples, Tainan will be a great destination. Travelers can not only visit temples, but also experience ancient Chinese traditions and age-old religious ceremonies. I will give them the best memories about Taiwan ever.

台灣是亞洲地理景觀與文化最多樣化的城市。台灣人有美麗的海灘、溫泉和夜市……等。旅行者總是能在台灣發現有趣的地方。如果要我推薦外國人台灣旅遊景點，我會先詢問他們的喜好，讓他們在有限的旅遊時間中能盡興。如果他們喜歡海灘，墾丁會是很棒的選擇。墾丁溫暖的熱帶氣候，成了冬天最受歡迎的景點；衝浪、浮潛是那裡最受歡迎的水上活動。若是喜歡廟宇，那台南就是很好的選擇。遊客不但能參觀古意盎然的廟宇，還能體驗傳統的宗教儀式。我相信我能為這些外國朋友留下最難忘的台灣體驗。

考試動機問題答題重點

　　永遠站在招募公司方思考，陳述自己能對公司有何貢獻。千萬別以自己的利益或想法為出發點。例如：喜歡旅遊、想環遊世界、趁年輕想到處體驗異文化、從小夢想成為一名空服員、增加人生閱歷等等。航空公司想要了解的是你有沒有成為優秀空服員的動機，喜歡旅遊是你的個人興趣，雖然與空服員的工作相關，但那是你的個人夢想，並無法讓主考官強烈感覺你適合成為一位空服員。

Q1
Track 34

Why do you want to be a flight attendant?
為什麼想成為一位空服員？

A1 I've always wanted to find a job which can dedicate myself to helping people. After evaluating my personality and ability, I found being a flight attendant is the best way for me to fulfill my dream. I can take a good care of passengers who take flights and travel with different purposes. In order to become a great flight attendant, I always train myself to handle emergencies by being equipped with possible solutions to various situations in advance. You won't be regretful to have me in your team.

　　我希望能選擇一份能幫助別人的工作。在評估自己的個性和能力後，我發現空服員是最能實現我夢想的工作。我相信我能照顧為了不同目的搭乘飛機和旅遊的乘客。為了能成為一位好的空服員，我總是讓自己事先準備好應付各種情況的解決方案，來訓練自己處理突發狀況的能力。選擇我成為您團隊的一員，相信您不會後悔的。

What part of being a flight attendant interests you most?
空服員這個職業的什麼部分最吸引你？

A2 Being a flight attendant allow you to meet lots of people. I think it's hard to find another job that can possibly to meet more people than a flight attendant. I enjoy communicating with people and hoping to help people. After evaluating my personality and ability, I find that being a flight attendant will be my vocation for life. I hope I can have an opportunity to be one member of your team and work for your esteemed company.

　　空服員這個職業最吸引我的地方是能夠遇見很多人，我想很難再找到另一個職業比空服員遇見的人更多。我喜歡接觸人、了解人、跟人相處，更希望能盡一己之力幫助其它人。評估了自己的能力和性格後，覺得空服員會是我人生的志業。希望能有這個機會成為貴公司團隊，為貴公司效力。

航空公司相關問題答題重點

在應試前，一定要仔細研讀應試公司的官方網站，了解公司的經營理念、VIP 制度、航班特色等等。同時加入應試公司的臉書等所有能獲得相關訊息的管道，注意相關新聞。

【實用英文句型】

As far as I know / To my knowledge 據我了解

Q1 Track 36

What do you think the difference between low fare airlines and traditional airlines?
你覺得廉價航空與傳統航空有何分別？

A1 Because I want to work in the airline industry, I used to take flights of low fare airlines and traditional airlines. In my opinion, I think if you want to understand something, you have to be really into it. Therefore, from my personal experience, every low fare and traditional airline has its own corporate culture and mission. The major difference will be air ticket fare and service items. For example, meal is not included in the air ticket fare of low fare airlines. Nevertheless, passengers will ask for the same service quality. Therefore, being a flight attendant, we have to use the same service standard and try our best to serve all passengers.

However, people might wonder why low fare airlines can offer low fare air ticket. I think that's because they come to a compromise in flight time, entertainment facilities and parking apron location. But with most of costs saved, the expense for the safe flights can't never be reduced since it is always the top priority for every airline, whether it's a low-fare or traditional one. Low fare airlines provide a chance to passengers to see the world and I think this is great.

　　因為想進入航空業，廉價航空與傳統航空我都搭乘過，因為我覺得凡事要親身體驗才能真正了解。從我自身體驗，我認為無論廉價航空或傳統航空，每家航空公司都有自己的企業文化與經營理念。廉價航空和傳統航空對旅客而言，最大的分別當然是價格與提供的服務項目。例如：餐點不包括在票價中等等，但是旅客對服務態度的要求是一樣的。所以作為空服員，服務旅客的心情和標準也是一樣。就我自己的搭乘經驗而言，廉價航空能有票價優勢，是省下在飛機上的娛樂設施、班機時間與機場的停機坪位置的妥協，但相信在航空安全上的費用是無法縮減的，因為飛安是每一家航空公司的第一考量，不論是廉航或傳統航空公司皆是如此。廉價航空的出現，是給予旅客一個不同的選擇，讓更多的人能有更多機會出國看世界，我覺得是一件很好的事情。

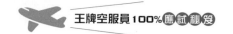

Q2
Track 37

To you, what's the most impressive public charities of China Airlines?

對華航印象最深刻的公益活動？

A2 As far as I know, China Airlines, considering the company as a member of the society, have made efforts in cooperating with other public institutions to engage in public charities. Apart from SARS, Iran earthquake, and the South Asian Tsunami, personally, the most impressive public charity is the donation of English books for the students in remote areas from year 2002. I think this is a very practical and meaningful charity activity. Education is an area that needs years-long establishment and its importance can't be easily ignored for every country. Meanwhile, English is an essential communication tool to open people's mind. Therefore, I have been greatly impressed by the donation of English books held by China Airlines.

據我了解，華航以身為企業公民為己任，以自有資源與其它專業機構合作做了許多國內外公益活動。除了 SARS、伊朗地震及南亞海嘯這些救災活動，我印象最深刻的是越洋募書活動。華航從 2002 年發起讓愛延伸活動，2003 年為台灣學童開啟英語學習之路，一直以來為偏遠學童越洋募集英文童書，我覺得這是非常實質且深具意義的公益活動。因為教育是百年大計，對一個國家尤其重要。而英語又是開啟人世界觀和與更多人溝通的必要工具。所以我對華航的越洋募書活動印象非常深刻。

To you, what's the most impressive public charities of Eva Air?

Track 38

對長榮印象最深刻的公益活動？

A3 To my knowledge, Eva air has the mission of Community Engagement and has put lots of efforts into local tourism constructions, sports and cultural activities. Personally, the most impressive public charity of Eva Air is the promotion and establishment of the local tourism. I think this is a very practical and meaningful charity activity. The charities will make more people fall in love with Taiwan. Therefore, I have been greatly impressed by Eva Air's efforts in the local tourism.

　　據我了解，長榮以社會共榮為己任，長期對地方回饋、體育賽事和藝文活動等不遺餘力。我印象最深刻的是長榮積極推動台灣觀光，參與各地方縣市政府的觀光活動，創造地方更多的觀光收入。我覺得這是非常實質且深具意義的公益活動。因為深耕台灣，讓台灣變得更好，使世界更多人喜歡台灣這片土地與文化，是最好的國民外交。所以我對長榮長期對地方觀光回饋活動印象非常深刻。

空服員相關問題答題重點

　　應試前需了解空服員的工作內容與生活，答題時給予心中完全以自己就是航空公司最佳選擇的心態，做正面回答。答題時以實例或數據回答能加強可信度。

Q1

Track 39

Some people think being flight attendant is very dangerous. Why do you want to choose this job?
有些人覺得機上工作非常危險,為什麼你要選擇這份工作?

A1 According to the statistics, the rate of aircraft accidents is 1/1,200,000, so it's safe transportation. As for why I want to be a flight attendant, I think my personality and ability are suitable for this job. I believe I can be a good flight attendant. A good flight attendant can assist passengers to have a comfortable flight in the airtight cabin with high pressure. I've also learned that some people might feel stressed during flights and it might be caused by a bad flight experience, scary flight stories, or uncomfortable body conditions. And this is when a good flight attendant shall show up to ease their discomfort. All in all, I think being a flight attendant is very meaningful. I hope I can have an opportunity to serve all passengers and offer them a pleasant journey.

據統計,飛機失事率只有 120 萬分之 1,是相對安全的交通運輸工具。我選擇這份工作是因為適合自己的性格和能力,我相信自己能勝任這份工作。空服員的工作能幫助旅客在機艙這個高壓,完全密閉空間中感覺自在。我也了解很多人在飛機上會感到壓力,可能是因為以往不愉快的飛行經驗,或聽到關於飛行的可怕故事,也可能是身體會覺得不適,而這就是空服員該現身,並紓緩乘客們不適的時候。總之,空服員是一份很有意義的工作;希望有機會能為所有旅客服務,給所有旅客一個美好的旅程。

Q2
Track 40

If a passenger has unreasonable requests, how will you handle it?

若是顧客有無理要求，你會如何處理？

A2 First, I will need to know and understand the definition of an unreasonable request. After all, we might have different definitions of unreasonable requests. I think this is also the best time to test the flight attendant's ability. If I face this kind of situation, I will listen carefully and show my empathy. At the same time, I will try to think the best solution I can offer. I think the reason why most people might have unreasonable requests is that they can't control their fury and don't know there is something cannot be done during flights. In my opinion, if I can ease their fury first and then fix their problems second, then I can deal with most unreasonable requests.

　　首先我會先了解無理要求的定義。畢竟每個人對於定義不合理的要求都不同，這時也是考驗一個空服員應變能力的時候。我會先仔細聆聽顧客的要求，並表示同理心，同時立刻在腦中思考最好的解決方式。我想大部分的顧客若是有無理要求，多半是無法控制一股怒氣，或是不了解在飛機上有些在地面上無法做到的事。我想先解決情緒，再解決問題後，我就能處理大部分無理的要求。

Q3

Track 41

Why should we hire you?

為什麼我們要錄取你？

A3 First of all, I appreciate the opportunity to be here and get a step closer to this job. After studying thoroughly the cabin crew requirements, I evaluated my personality and ability carefully. I have confidence to do this job well. I believe that all things are not that tough if I put my heart into them. My ability, personality, confidence and willingness are reasons why you should hire me. I know it's not easy to be your team member, but if I have an opportunity, I will try my best to meet the requirements of your company.

首先，我要謝謝貴公司給我這個機會讓我能在這裡爭取這個我夢想中的工作。我在看了貴公司所需要的組員條件，仔細評估了自己的能力與人格特質，我有信心能勝任這份工作。我一直相信，天下無難事，只怕有心人。我想能力、性格、自信和意願是貴公司能放心錄取我的原因，我有自信也有心投入這份工作。我知道想加入貴公司的團隊不易，但如果能有機會，我一定會盡力做到最好，不負公司期望。

Q4

Track 42

If you have to be on duty on New Year's Eve, how will you feel?

如果你被排到除夕夜上班，你的心情會是如何？

A4 I think everyone has the different definition about New Year's

Eve. In my opinion, I think every day is a special day. Therefore, I think that day matters. If my colleague would like to spend time with her family on New Year's Eve, I am willing to change my duty with her. Moreover, I think it is going to be a different experience to spend time with all passengers and crew on New Year's Eve during the flight.

　　每個人對過節的意義不同。我覺得每一天都是特別的一天，所以除夕夜當然也很特別。如果有同事除夕夜想與家人一同過節，我也會很願意跟她換班。而且跟全飛機上的人一同過除夕夜，也是一種不同的體驗。

Q5

Track 43

Are you willing to be based wherever the company sends you?

你願意接受公司安排你的派遣地嗎？

A5 Yes, I am. The essence of this job is cosmopolitan. People who can feel at home wherever they go are suitable for this job. I left home since I went to the university and felt free to be independent. I think I can adapt to different environments easily. Furthermore, if I work for the airline, it's not a big problem to go home whenever I have time.

　　我願意。空服員這個職業本來就是以四海為家，無論派遣至何地，都能適應的人，才適合空服工作，而且現在航空那麼發達，我又是在航空公司工作，想回家不是難事。更何況我從大學就已經離開家在外求學工作，很能適應環境與一個人的生活。

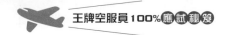

Q6

Track 44

Have you ever heard any stories about flight attendants? Please share with us.

你聽過什麼有關空服員的事嗎？ 請跟我們分享。

A6 People usually have an imagination about flight attendants. To them, they all are good looking and living a glamorous life, like having breakfast in Paris today and dinner in New York next week. However, I have different viewpoints. Flight attendants need to require certain abilities, including high EQ and strong resilience. My friend who is a flight attendant once shared her experience with me. Here it is: she met a pregnant passenger who had miscarriage during the flight to New York. At that time, flight attendants on the airplane had to be calm and handled the situation immediately. After hearing this story, I want myself to be decisive when handling everything firmly and quickly. Since being a good flight attendant, he/she won't have much time to think when facing emergencies.

　　許多人對空服員的想像是光鮮亮麗，每天在不同國家旅行，今天在巴黎吃早餐，下週到紐約吃晚餐。但我有不同的想法，對我而言，空服員是需要高 EQ、高應變能力才能勝任的。我聽過當空服員的朋友在飛往紐約的班機上，在高空飛行時孕婦小產，必須立即處理。自聽到這件事後，我在日常生活處理事情時，會要求自己處事明快，以符合做為空服員資格，畢竟碰上這樣的緊急狀況，空服員是沒有太多時間可以思考的。

What do you think a flight attendant does?
你覺得空服員的工作內容是什麼？

Track 45

A7 Taking a good care of passengers from boarding to getting off a plane is the major part of job for flight attendants. Airline company has planned the entire service procedure and keep the service quality great for passengers. All I have to do is try my best to reach the company standard and offer every passenger a great journey.

　　空服員的工作內容就是照顧旅客，從登機到旅客離開飛機。公司已經為所有乘客規劃出一整套的服務流程，並維持最好的服務品質。我能做的，是盡力達到公司標準，讓每位旅客都能有最好的空中體驗。

How does one be a good flight attendant?
如何成為一位好的空服員？

Track 46

A8 A good flight attendant should be friendly and polite to everyone. Nice grooming and elegant behaviors are basic criteria. Always smiling is the key. Always leave your personal emotions at home instead of taking them with you to work. We must be a great company ambassador and deliver the company spirit to passengers. Punctuality is very important as flights cannot wait for us.

　　Security is crucial. We should always follow company's SOP to

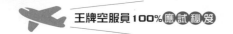
check safety of every item. Never take any chance. Team work is very important. We should help each other whether we are in flights or overseas. Personal integrity is necessary. We cannot take anything from flights, even just a can of soda or magazines. To be a flight attendant, one should be resourceful and having a strong mind. Here I would like to share my personal experience about a great flight attendant I had met during my flight to Bangkok. During the boarding time, a little boy vomited in the aisle. I saw the flight attendant came to comfort him immediately and gave him tissues. After that, she went to a galley to get a coffee bag and spread coffee powders on the carpet. I think she is the role model for being a great flight attendant.

　　一位好的空服員總是友善且有禮貌地對待所有人。良好的妝扮與優雅的儀態是基本要求。時時面帶微笑是重要關鍵。永遠不能將個人情緒帶入工作。我們必須成為公司的品牌大使，讓每位顧客感受到公司欲傳達的精神。準時是必須的，畢竟飛機是不等人的。個人操守是必要條件。絕不能將飛機上的任何物品帶下飛機，即使只是一瓶可樂或雜誌。安全十分重要。在登機準備時，務必檢查所有安全設備，千萬不能存有僥倖心態。無論在飛機上或是在外站，團隊合作是非常重要的。一位好的空服員必須有堅強的意志與絕佳應變能力，畢竟在飛機上什麼事都有可能發生。在此我想分享一個我個人搭機經驗。有次我搭機至曼谷，在登機時，有位小男孩突然吐在走道上。那位空服員立刻上前安慰小朋友，並拿面紙給他。然後至廚房拿出咖啡包，將咖啡粉蓋在走道的嘔吐物上以繼續完成登機作業。在我心中，她是一位優良空服員典範。

Q9
Track 47

If you and your family quarrel before boarding, what will you do?

在飛行前跟家人起口角怎麼辦？

A9 In my opinion, leaving all personal matters at home when being at work is the basic rule for every career, especially for flight attendants. Being a flight attendant, high concentration and emotion management are essential requirements. Most passengers don't get used to stay in high-altitude pressure; some unusual situations might happen during flights. Therefore, as a professional flight attendant, I will ask myself to have great performance when I am on duty. Moreover, when I am off duty, my family and I might have already left the quarrel behind.

公歸公，私歸私，我是不會把私人情緒帶到工作的，這是基本的工作禮儀。尤其空服員是個需要高度專注力與情緒管理的工作，一般旅客不習慣處於高空壓力中，許多狀況都有可能在飛行中發生。身為專業的空服員，要求自己以最好狀態工作是必須的。所以我會先把私事放下，專注工作。更何況事緩則圓，等我結束工作時，家人和我可能都不記得這件事了。

応試前準備 ❶
応試技巧 ❷
飛上青空情境大模擬 ❸

面試題庫整理
❼ 其它問題

答題重點

　　考官有時會提出比較與選擇航空公司問題，這時你必須表情堅定，明確選擇，但不毀損任何一個選項，同時將答案與應試工作結合。

　　若遇到負面或涉及你不想提及的部分提問時，一定要微笑以對，以正面態度及語句作答。先認同主考官的問題，再提出自己的論述，千萬不要否決主考官的問題。

實用英文句型

我同意您的觀點 I agree with your opinion

是的 That's true.

我絕對贊成您 I couldn't agree with you more.

我完全贊同 I agree completely.

對的 Exactly.

我會將其認為 I will consider that

事實上 Actually

If you get offers from two airlines companies, which company will you choose?

如果同時有兩家航空公司錄取你，你會選哪一家？

A1 It will be my great honor to get two offers in the airline industry. I will consider that I am very suitable for being a flight attendant. Actually, I did full research of companies' cultures and requirements, and evaluated my abilities to see if I was the one they need before participating in any recruitment. If I consider myself not suitable for the company, I won't apply for the position. Therefore, if I have the great honor to get offers from two companies, I will be very grateful and re-evaluate myself to see which company I can contribute more.

很榮幸有兩家航空公司同時錄取我，表示我真的非常適合空服員這個職業。在選擇應試每家航空公司前，我都已經好好研究過航空公司的文化與要求，認真評估自己的能力，考慮自己是否是該航空公司要的人才。若我覺得自己無法符合該航空公司的文化與要求，我就不會去應試。因此，如果我有這個榮幸讓兩家公司同時錄取我，我會懷著感恩的心，在兩家我都很喜愛的公司重新評估自己能為哪家公司貢獻更多。

1 應試前準備

2 應試技巧

3 飛上青空情境大模擬

Q2
Track 49

Did you participate in other airline's recruitment activities? If you don't get the offer, what will be the reason?

是否有去其它航空公司面試？若沒有被錄取，你覺得會是什麼原因？

A2 I choose being a flight attendant as my occupation. And the requirements of flight attendants for each company might differ due to its culture. To be qualified as a flight attendant, I chose companies that are suitable for me after the evaluation. I made my evaluation carefully; however, sometimes the evaluation fails. If I don't get the offer, it doesn't mean I will not be a good flight attendant. It just means my personality or ability are not suitable for the company I interviewed with. Thus, I will keep trying my best to become a flight attendant.

空服員是我為自己選擇的職業，而每家航空公司因其公司文化，對空服員的要求不盡相同；為了能成為空服員，我選擇了我評估後適合我的航空公司面試。雖然我的每次評估都很謹慎，但還是有疏失的時候，若沒有被錄取，並不是我不適合空服員這個職業，而是與去面試的航空公司文化不同。我會繼續努力成為一名空服員。

Q3
Track 50

What's the difference between China Airlines and Eva Air? What will you choose?

長榮和華航有何不同？你會怎麼選擇？

A3 I think China Airlines and Eve Air are totally different, no matter in their company culture, and the style of management. Before deciding to participate in this recruitment, I have done a full research. Now I am here not there because I have confidence to be one of your excellent team members.

長榮和華航是完全不同的航空公司，無論在文化、經營理念各方面。我在應試前，仔細研究了兩家公司的文化，現在我站在這裡而不是另一間公司，表示我有自信成為貴公司優秀團隊的一員，為貴公司服務。

1 應試前準備

2 應試技巧

3 飛上青空情境大模擬

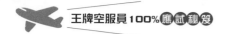

Q4 Track 51

Your figure is plump. Do you think you will look good in a flight attendant uniform?

你的身型似乎比較偏胖，你覺得穿空服制服會好看嗎？

A4 You are right. I am not skinny. However, I think I have a well-proportioned shape. Not to mention your flight attendant uniform is suitable for every figure. I believe I will be a charming flight attendant once I wear the uniform. I hope I can have an opportunity to wear your uniform. I believe you will think the same.

您說得對，我不是纖瘦型身材，但我身材的比例好，加上貴公司的制服剪裁和樣式很適合各種身型，我覺得自己穿起來一定好看。希望您能給我機會穿上貴公司制服，相信您也會贊成我的想法。

Q5 Track 52

Your skin is quite dark. Do you think you look like a flight attendant?

你的膚色偏黑，你覺得自己看起來像空服員嗎？

A5 You are right. I am not a snow white. However, healthy skin is the sublimation of being dynamic and healthy. I believe passengers will appreciate various styles that flight attendants present.

您說得對，我不是白皙膚色的女生，但我覺得像我這樣健康膚色的女生，更能讓旅客感受到空服員的健康與活力。我相信旅客會喜歡看到各種不同類型的空服員樣貌。

Q6
Track 53

Your grades are not good. Do you think you can be a good flight attendant?

你在校成績不是很理想,你覺得自己能成為好的空服員嗎?

A6 You are right. My grade in the school is not good. However, I believe I can be a good flight attendant as my personality is suitable for being a flight attendant. I am outgoing and independent; I enjoy working with people and working efficiently. And I am a decisive person as well. I am always happy to face any challenges.

您說得對,我在校成績不是很理想,但我相信自己絕對能成為一位好的空服員,因為我的個性非常適合空服員工作。我個性外向獨立,喜歡與陌生人接觸,處事有效率且果斷,樂於接受挑戰。

PART 3 飛上青空情境大模擬

機艙廣播詞

❶ 登機與起飛前廣播詞

登機相關廣播

Track 54

登機廣播 (Pre-flight announcement)

Attention please. Ladies and gentlemen, this is the pre-boarding announcement for flight 111 to Bangkok. We are now inviting those passengers with small children, and any passengers requiring special assistance, to begin boarding at this time. Please have your boarding pass and passport ready. Regular boarding will begin in approximately ten minutes time. Thank you for your cooperation.

中文翻譯

　　請注意！各位貴賓您好，這是 111 班次飛往曼谷的登機廣播。我們現在邀請有孩童同行、需要特別協助的旅客開始登機，請先將您的登機證和護照準備好。其它旅客大約在 10 分鐘後登機。感謝您的合作。

Track 55

最後登機廣播 (Final Pre-flight announcement)

Attention please. This is the final boarding call for passengers Miss Tsai Ling Ling booked on flight 111 to New York. Please proceed to gate 6 immediately. The final checks are being completed and the captain will order the doors of the aircraft to close in approximately five minutes time. Thank you.

中文翻譯

　　請注意！搭乘 111 班次前往紐約的旅客蔡靈靈小姐，這是您最後的登機廣播。請立即至 6 號登機門登機。機長將會在約 5 分鐘後關閉艙門，謝謝！

航班延誤廣播（Flight delay announcement）

Track 56

飛機保養造成延誤 (Delay due to aircraft maintenance)

Attention please. Winner Airlines regrets to announce that the departure of flight number AB111 to Bangkok is delayed due to aircraft maintenance. The new boarding time will be 3:00 pm. We apologize for the inconvenience and thank you for your patience.

中文翻譯

　　請注意！由於飛機保養緣故，Winner 航空前往曼谷的班機 AB111 將延誤，新的登機時間將會在下午 3 點。造成您的不便敬請見諒，感謝您的耐心。

Track 57

保養後登機廣播 (Boarding announcement)

Attention please. Ladies and gentlemen, we apologize for the delay. The technical problems have been solved. We would like to thank you for your patience and cooperation. We are now ready for boarding.

中文翻譯

請注意！各位貴賓您好！很抱歉造成班機延誤，目前飛機保養已經完成。非常感謝您的耐心與合作。現在我們準備登機。

Track 58

航道擁擠造成延誤 (Delay due to air traffic congestion announcement)

Attention please. Ladies and gentlemen, this is your captain speaking. We are now fully ready for departure; however, due to air traffic congestion in Hong Kong , we are given a departure clearance time of 3 PM. This is beyond our control. We sincerely apologize for the inconvenience brought about by this delay.

中文翻譯

請注意！各位貴賓您好，這是機長廣播。我們現在已經做好起飛準備，但由於目前香港機場航道擁擠，我們被安排在下午 3 點起飛。對於這個我們無法控制因素所造成的延誤，在此向您表達誠摯的歉意。

Track 59

航班起飛廣播 (Take off announcement)

Ladies and gentlemen, we have been informed by the control tower that we can take off now. We apologize for the delay and would like to thank you for your patience and cooperation. We are now ready for take-off.

中文翻譯

　　請注意！各位貴賓您好！機場塔台已經告知我們現在可以請飛。很抱歉造成班機延誤，非常感謝您的耐心與合作。現在我們準備起飛。

機艙內起飛前廣播 (In flight Boarding announcement)
Ladies and gentlemen, the Captain has turned on the Fasten Seat Belt sign. Please stow your carry-on luggage underneath the seat in front of you or in an overhead bin. Please take your seat and fasten your seat belt. And also make sure your seat back and folding trays are in their full upright position. If you are seated next to an emergency exit, please read carefully the special instructions card located by your seat.

At this time, we request that all personal electronic devices should be turned off during taking off and landing, as these items might interfere with the navigational and communication equipment on this aircraft. We request that all other electronic devices be turned off until we fly above 10,000 feet. We will notify you when it is safe to use such devices.

We remind you that this is a non-smoking flight. Smoking is prohibited on the entire aircraft, including the lavatories. Tampering with, disabling or destroying the lavatory smoke detector is

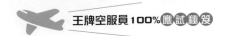
prohibited by law.

If you have any questions about our flight today, please don't hesitate to ask one of our flight attendants. We wish you a pleasant journey. We are now ready to take off.

中文翻譯

各位貴賓您好,機長已經將請繫安全帶的指示燈開啟。請將您的隨身行李放置在座位前下方或座位上方的置物箱。同時繫好您的安全帶,並將您的椅背豎直、桌子收起,若您的座位在逃生出口旁,請仔細閱讀座位前方特別的安全指示卡。

同時,在起飛與降落時,請將您的個人電子用品關機,以免影響飛航安全。在飛機到達高空一萬呎後,我們會通知您能使用您的個人電子用品。

在此提醒您這是禁煙班機,在飛機上的任何地方都不能吸煙,包括洗手間在內。觸動洗手間的煙霧偵測器是違法行為。

若您對我們今天的航班有任何疑問,請隨時與我們空服組員聯繫。祝您有個愉快的旅程。

Track 61

機艙關門 (Door closure)

Ladies and gentlemen, my name is Lillian and I am your flight attendant. On behalf of Captain Charles and the entire crew, welcome aboard Victory Airline flight NXO, from Taiwan to Paris.

Our flight time will be 13 hours and 50 minutes. We will be flying at an altitude of 10,000 feet at a ground speed of 800 miles per hour. At this time, make sure your seat backs and tray tables are in their full upright position. Also make sure your seat belt is correctly fastened. Also, we advise you that as of this moment, any electronic equipment must be turned off. Thank you.

中文翻譯

　　各位貴賓您好，我是今天為您服務的空服員 Lillian，在此代表今天的機長 Charles 與全體組員，歡迎您搭乘 Victory 航空 NXO 班機，由台灣飛往巴黎。

　　我們今天的飛行時間將是 13 小時 50 分。飛航高度為 10,000 呎，飛行速度是每小時 800 哩。

　　現在請將您椅背豎直，桌子收好，同時確認您已繫好安全帶。所有的電子用品請關機，謝謝！

機上安全示範（Safety demonstration）

Track 62

有安全示範影片 (Safety demonstration film)

Ladies and gentlemen, I'd like to direct your attention to the television monitors. We will be showing our safety demonstration and would like the next few minutes of your complete attention.

中文翻譯

各位貴賓您好，我們將播放機上安全示範影片，請仔細觀看。

Track 63

空服員示範 (Live Safety demonstration)

Ladies and gentlemen, now we request your full attention as the flight attendants demonstrate the safety features of this aircraft.

When the seat belt sign illuminates, you must fasten your seat belt. Insert the metal fittings on into the other, and tighten by pulling on the loose end of the strap. To release your seat belt, lift the upper portion of the buckle. We suggest that you keep your seat belt fastened throughout the flight, as we may experience turbulence. There are several emergency exits on this aircraft. Please take a few moments now to locate your nearest exit. In some cases, your nearest exit may be behind you. If you need to evacuate the aircraft, floor-level lighting will guide you towards the exit. Doors can be opened by moving the handle in the direction of the arrow. Each door is equipped with an inflatable slide which may also be detached and used as a life raft.

Oxygen and air pressure are always being monitored. In the event of a decompression, an oxygen mask will automatically appear in front of you. To start the flow of oxygen, pull the mask towards you. Place it firmly over your nose and mouth, secure the elastic band behind your head, and breathe normally. Although the bag does not inflate, oxygen is flowing to the mask. If you are travelling with a child or someone who requires assistance, secure your mask on first, and then assist the other person. Keep your mask on until a uniformed crew member advises you to remove it.

In the event of an emergency, please assume the bracing position. (Lean forward with your hands on top of your head and your elbows against your thighs. Ensure your feet are flat on the floor.) A life vest is located in a pouch under your seat or between the armrests. When instructed to do so, open the plastic pouch and remove the vest. Slip it over your head. Pass the straps around your waist and adjust at the front. To inflate the vest, pull firmly on the red cord, only when leaving the aircraft. If you need to refill the vest,

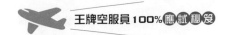
blow into the mouthpieces. Use the whistle and light to attract attention. (Also, your seat bottom cushion can be used as a flotation device. Pull the cushion from the seat, slip your arms into the straps, and hug the cushion to your chest.)

At this time, your portable electronic devices must be set to 'airplane' mode until an announcement is made upon arrival.

We remind you that this is a non-smoking flight. Tampering with, disabling, or destroying the smoke detectors located in the lavatories is prohibited by law.

You will find this and all the other safety information in the card located in the seat pocket in front of you. We strongly suggest you read it before take-off. If you have any questions, please don't hesitate to ask one of our crew members. We wish you all an enjoyable flight.

Flight attendants, prepare for take-off please.
Cabin crew, please take your seats for take-off.

中文翻譯

各位貴賓您好，空服員現在將為您做機上安全示範，請您仔細觀看。

當繫上安全帶的指示燈亮起時，請務必繫好您的安全帶。將安全帶的一端放入扣環中，並將安全帶調整至適當鬆緊度。若要解開安全帶，只需

將安全帶扣環往上即可。建議您在飛行中隨時繫上安全帶，以避免可能遇到的亂流。

機上有多個緊急出口，請留意最靠近您的出口。若需要緊急疏散，地面上的燈號會指示您到達緊急出口。

只要依照機艙門的箭頭移動門把，機艙門即可打開。每個機艙門都配備充氣滑梯，若遇到水上迫降可當作救生艇使用。

機上的氧氣與氣壓都調適在您最舒適的狀態。若機艙失壓時，氧氣面罩會自動出現在您面前。您只需拉下氧氣面罩罩住口鼻，調整好鬆緊度，然後正常呼吸即可。您不會看到氧氣面罩膨脹，但氧氣會自動進入您的面罩中。若您與孩童貨需要您協助的人同行，請先戴好您的氧氣面罩，再協助旁人。請一直戴著氧氣面罩等候空服組員的指示。

在緊急迫降時，請確實做好前抱（彎腰抱頭）姿勢。（頭部盡量向前傾，將雙手放在頭上，手肘抵住大腿，並確保您的雙腳平放在地板上。）

在您的座位下方或扶手之間有救生衣，這是兩面都可以使用的。使用時請先將救生衣由頭部套入，將後面的兩條腰帶拉到前面扣上扣環，拉緊腰帶。救生衣下方有兩個紅色拉環，向下一拉即會自動充氣，請在離開飛機後再充氣。救生衣夾層有兩條紅色吹管，如不能自動充氣或需要再充氣，請直接向裡面吹氣，直到充滿空氣為止。在水中請使用口哨和燈光吸引注意。您的座位底部緩衝墊同時能當作漂浮裝置，將坐墊座位拉出，將手臂放入繩中，將胸部靠在坐墊上抱住坐墊。

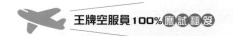

同時,您的隨身攜帶發電裝置必須設在「飛機」模式,直到聽到抵達的廣播。在這個時候,你的便攜式電子設備必須設置為「飛機」模式,直至公告抵達時。

提醒您這是禁煙班機。亂動、阻塞或破壞洗手間的煙霧偵測器是觸犯法律行為。

所有安全資訊都在您座位前方的袋中。我們鄭重建議您於起飛前閱讀。若您有任何問題,請隨時詢問我們任何一位空服組員。希望您有個愉快的旅程!

空服組員,請準備起飛。
空服組員,請就座準備起飛。

到達安全高度 (Release seat belts)

Track 64

Ladies and gentlemen, the Captain has turned off the Fasten Seat Belt sign, and you may now move around the cabin. However, we always recommend you keep your seat belt fastened while you're seated. You may now turn on your electronic devices such as calculators, CD players, and laptop computers.
In a few moments, the flight attendants will be passing around the cabin to offer you hot or cold drinks, as well as breakfast/supper/a snack/a light meal. Alcoholic drinks are also available with our compliments. Enjoy the flight. Thank you.

　　各位貴賓您好，機長已將請繫安全帶的指示燈熄滅，您現在可在機艙內自由走動。我們仍建議您在座位上時，隨時繫好您的安全帶。您現在可以使用您的個人電子用品。

　　再幾分鐘，空服員將為您準備飲料，在此航程中，我們也將為您準備早餐／點心／輕食。含酒精飲料也是免費提供，祝您有個美好旅程，謝謝。

到達安全高度後的廣播詞

Track 65

發送入境表格 (Distributing customs forms announcement) Ladies and gentlemen, we will begin distributing customs forms to you shortly. If you have any questions, please contact our flight attendants. Thank you.

中文翻譯

　　各位貴賓您好，我們將發送入境表格，若您有任何疑問，請告知我們空服組員，謝謝！

娛樂服務廣播（Entertainment Service announcement）

雜誌位置 (Magazine)

For your enjoyment during our flight today, we have placed a complimentary copy of our in-flight magazine in the seat pocket in front of you. If you wish, please feel free to take this with you when you leave.

中文翻譯

在您的座位前方袋中備有機上雜誌伴您享受您的旅程。歡迎您在離機時將它帶走。

機上免稅銷售 (In flight Shopping)

Those interested in buying duty free goods will also find our Duty Shop Catalog in the seat pocket in front of you.

You will find controls for your reading light, call button and the in flight entertainment system on the inside of your seat armrest. To adjust your seat, push the round button beside the panel. The lavatories are located at the front, middle and rear of these cabins.

Tea, coffee and a full bar service will be available throughout the flight. If you require any special assistance, please contact the flight attendant nearest you. We are here to ensure that you have a comfortable and enjoyable flight. Later on we'll dim the cabin lights so you can get some rest. We recommend that while sleeping, you keep your seatbelt fastened over the top of your blanket. This way it will not be necessary to wake you up should the seatbelt sign come on during the flight. If you don't want to be woken up for breakfast, please advice a flight attendant.

中文翻譯

您可以在您座位前方袋中的免稅品目錄找到您喜愛的免稅品。

閱讀燈、服務鈴及機上娛樂系統可在您座位把手中的遙控器控制。若您想調整座椅位置，只需輕按座椅旁按鈕。飛機的前方、中間與後方均設有洗手間。

機上提供茶、咖啡及酒吧服務，若您需要任何特別協助，請告知您最近的空服員。我們將確保您有個舒適愉快的旅程。稍後我們會將機艙燈光調暗方便您休息。我們建議您在入睡前將安全帶繫在毛毯上，這樣當繫上安全帶指示燈亮起時，您就不會被打擾。若您不想被喚醒使用早餐，請告知空服組員。

亂流 (Turbulence)

Track 68

Ladies and gentlemen, the captain has turned on the fasten seat belt sign. We are now crossing a zone of turbulence. Please returned your seats and keep your seat belts fastened. Thank you.

Flight attendants/ Cabin crew, please be seated.

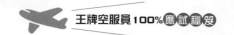
中文翻譯

各位貴賓您好，機長已經將請繫安全帶的指示燈開啟，我們目前正進入亂流區。請回到您的座位，並將您的安全帶繫好。謝謝！

空服組員請就座。

Track 69

飛機下降 (Descent)

We hope you have enjoyed the in-flight entertainment. We are now preparing to land. The bar is closed and we will soon collect your headsets. May I remind you to complete your arrival and immigration documentation by the time we arrive at the airport.

Ladies and gentlemen, as we start our descent, please make sure your seat backs and tray tables are in their full upright position. Make sure your seat belt is securely fastened and all carry-on luggage is stowed underneath the seat in front of you or in the overhead bins. Please turn off all electronic devices until we are safely parked at the gate. Thank you.

Flight attendants, prepare for landing please.
Cabin crew, please take your seats for landing.

中文翻譯

我們希望您享受機上娛樂系統，現在飛機準備降落。飲料服務將關閉，同時很快將收回您的耳機。提醒您在到達機場前完成所有入境表格。

各位貴賓您好，我們現在開始下降。請確定您將椅背豎直，桌子收好，同時請繫好安全帶。所有隨身行李請放置在座位前下方或座位上方置物櫃。請將您所有個人電子用品關機，謝謝。

空服組員，請準備降落。
空服組員，請就座準備降落。

memo

1　應試前準備

2　應試技巧

3　飛上青空情境大模擬

機艙廣播詞
❸ 目的地政府規定廣播與其他廣播

目的地政府規定廣播
（Destination government rules announcement）

Track 70

美國（USA）

Ladies and gentlemen, all arriving passengers must complete a customs declaration form. May we remind you that passengers carrying fruits, vegetables, meats, plants, seeds, or related agricultural products are reminded to declare those items. There is no limit on the amount of money that can be taken out of or brought into the United States. However, if you or your family travelling together have more than US$10,000 or its equivalent in foreign currency or marketable securities, you are required to declare this with Customs. Thank you.

中文翻譯

　　各位貴賓您好，所有入境美國旅客都必須填寫海關申報。在此提醒您，您所攜帶的水果、蔬菜、肉類、植物、種子或相關農產品都必須申報。入境美國所攜帶的金額並無限制。但如果您或您一家人攜帶超過美金一萬元以上，包括等值外國貨幣或有價證券，您需要與海關申報，謝謝。

新加坡（Singapore）

Ladies and gentlemen, according to regulations of the Singapore government, we are required to make the following announcement: The trafficking and importation of illegal drugs is a serious offense and the mandatory penalty for such is" death".Thank you for your attention.

中文翻譯

各位貴賓您好，根據新加坡政府規定，我們必須在機上進行下列廣播：非法走私或進口毒品是嚴重犯罪行為，最重將處以死刑。謝謝您的注意！

降落（Landing）

Ladies and gentlemen, welcome to Bangkok international airport. Local time is 3pm and the temperature is 30 degrees centigrade.

For your safety and comfort, please remain seated with your seat belt fastened until the Captain turns off the Fasten Seat Belt sign. This will indicate that we have parked at the gate and that it is safe for you to move about.

Please check around your seat for any personal belongings you may have brought on board with you and please use caution when opening the overhead bins, as heavy articles may have shifted around

during the flight.

If you require deplaning assistance, please remain in your seat until all other passengers have deplaned. One of our crew members will then be pleased to assist you.

We remind you to please wait until you are inside the terminal to use any electronic devices.

On behalf of Victory Airlines and the entire crew, I'd like to thank you for joining us on this trip, and we are looking forward to seeing you on board again in the near future. Have a nice day!

中文翻譯

各位貴賓您好，歡迎來到曼谷國際機場。當地時間是下午 3 點，地面溫度為攝氏 30 度。

為了您的安全與舒適，在機長將請繫安全帶的指示燈熄滅前，請留在您的座位上，並繫好安全帶。

在打開座位上方的置物櫃時，請特別注意，避免行李滑落下來。下機前，請檢查座位，別忘了個人隨身物品。

若您需要任何離機協助，請先留在您的座位，等其它旅客下機後，我們的空服組員將會立刻協助您。

提醒您在進入航廈前，不要使用任何個人電子用品。

在此代表 Victory 航空及全體組員，感謝您搭乘本班機。期待能很快再見到您。祝您有個美好的一天。

其它服務（Other services）

Wheelchair service is available for departing, arriving , transfer and transit passengers at each airport. If you need the wheelchair service, please let us know when you make the reservation or at least 24 hours before you travel. When travelling in a group of 10 or more passengers who use wheelchairs, please provide at least 48 hours of advance notice so that we can better assist you and provide the necessary stowage space.

中文翻譯

　　在每個機場都提供輪椅服務，無論在出境、入境、轉機等所有時刻。若您需要輪椅服務，請在您旅行前 24 小時預訂。若您的團體中有超過 10 人以上需要輪椅服務，請您於旅行前 48 小時預訂，讓我們能為您做最好的安排。

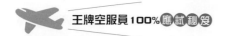

附錄　Appendix

主要城市與城市（機場）代碼

港澳及台灣地區		
國家	城市	城市（機場）代碼
台灣（Taiwan）	台北（Taipei）	TPE
台灣（Taiwan）	高雄（Kaohsiung）	KHH
中國（China）	香港（Hong Kong）	HKG
中國（China）	澳門（Macao）	MFM
大陸地區		
中國（China）	北京（Beijing）	PEK
中國（China）	上海（Shanghai）	SHA
中國（China）	天津（Tianjin）	TSN
中國（China）	西安（Xian）	SIA
中國（China）	杭州（Hangchow）	HGH
中國（China）	大連（Dalian）	DLC
中國（China）	青島（Tsingtao）	TAO
中國（China）	福州（Foochow）	FOC
中國（China）	廈門（Xiamen）	XMN
中國（China）	昆明（Kunming）	KMG
中國（China）	南京（Nanking）	NKG
中國（China）	汕頭（Swatow）	SWA
中國（China）	桂林（Guilin）	KWL
中國（China）	成都（Chengtu）	CTU
中國（China）	廣州（Canchow）	CAN
中國（China）	海口（Haikou）	HAK
中國（China）	長沙（Changsha）	CSX
中國（China）	煙台（Yantai）	YNT

中國（China）	重慶（Chongqing）	CKG
中國（China）	溫州（Wenzhou）	WNZ
中國（China）	三亞（Sanya）	SYX
中國（China）	哈爾濱（Harbin）	HRB
中國（China）	深圳（Shengzhen）	SZX
中國（China）	南昌（Nanchang）	KHN
東南亞地區		
泰國（Thailand）	曼谷（Bangkok）	BKK
泰國（Thailand）	清邁（Chiang Mai）	CNX
泰國（Thailand）	普吉島（Phuket）	HKT
馬來西亞（Malaysia）	吉隆坡（Kuala Lunpur）	KUL
馬來西亞（Malaysia）	檳城（Penang）	PEN
馬來西亞（Malaysia）	怡保（IPOH）	IPH
馬來西亞（Malaysia）	古晉（Kuching）	KCH
新加坡（Singapore）	新加坡（Singapore）	SIN
印尼（Indonesia）	雅加達（Jakarta）	JKT
印尼（Indonesia）	巴里島（Denpasar）	DPS
印尼（Indonesia）	棉蘭（Medan）	MES
印尼（Indonesia）	巨港（Palembang）	PLM
印尼（Indonesia）	泗水（Surabaya）	SUB
緬甸（Myanmar）	仰光（Rangoon）	RGN
越南（Vietnam）	河內（Hanoi）	HAN
越南（Vietnam）	金邊（Phnom Penh）	PNH
越南（Vietnam）	西貢（Saigon）	SGN
越南（Vietnam）	永珍（Vientiane）	VTE
菲律賓（Philippines）	馬尼拉（Manila）	MNL
菲律賓（Philippines）	宿霧（CEBU）	CEB
東帝汶（East Timor）	帝力（Dili）	DIL
馬來西亞（Malaysia）	亞庇（Kota Kinabalu）	BKI

孟加拉（Bangladesh）	達卡（Dacca）	DAC
馬拉西亞（Malaysia）	詩鄔（Sibu）	SBW
美國（U.S.A）	塞班（Saipan）	SPN
汶萊 （Brunei Darussalam）	斯里巴加灣市（Bander Seri Begawan）	BWN
印度（India）	新德里（New Delhi）	DEL
阿富汗（Afghanistan）	喀布爾（Kabul）	KBL
孟加拉（Bangladesh）	吉大港（Chittagon）	CGP
巴基斯坦（Pakistan）	喀拉蚩（Karachi）	KHI
東加王國（Tonga）	東加大埔（Tonggatapu）	TBU
諾魯（Nauru）	諾魯（Nauru）	INU
菲律賓（Philippines）	碧港（Baguio）	BAG
印度（India）	孟買（Bombay）	BOM
斯里蘭卡（Sri Lanka）	可倫坡（Colomba）	CMB
印度（India）	加爾各答（Calcutta）	CCU
印度（India）	馬德拉斯（Madras）	MAA
印度（India）	加得滿都（Kathmandu）	KTM
東北亞地區		
韓國（Korea）	釜山（Pusan）	PUS
韓國（Korea）	漢城（Seoul）	SEL
日本（Japan）	東京（Tokyo）	TYO
日本（Japan）	大阪（Osaka）	OSA
日本（Japan）	名古屋（Nagoya）	NGO
日本（Japan）	札幌（Sapporo）	SPK
日本（Japan）	福岡（Fukuoka）	FUK
日本（Japan）	沖繩（Okinawa）	OKA
中南美洲地區		
墨西哥（Mexico）	墨西哥（Mexico City）	Mex
薩爾瓦多（Salvador）	聖薩爾瓦多 （San Salvador）	SAL

巴拿馬（Panama）	巴拿馬（Panama City）	PTY
古巴（Cuba）	哈瓦那（Havana）	BOG
哥倫比亞（Colombia）	波哥大（Bogota）	UIO
厄瓜多共和國（Ecuador）	基多（Quito）	LIM
祕魯（Peru）	利馬（Lima）	SCL
智利（Chile）	聖地牙哥（Santiago）	SAN
阿根廷（Argentina）	布宜諾艾利斯（Buends Aires）	BUE
巴西（Brazil）	聖保羅（San Paulo）	SAO
巴西（Brazil）	里約熱內盧（Rio de Janeiro）	RIO
巴西（Brazil）	巴西利亞（Brassilia）	BSB
委內瑞拉（Venezuela）	加拉加斯（Caracas）	CCS
法國（France）	開雪（Cayenne）	CAY
烏拉圭（Uruguay）	蒙地維多（Montebideo）	MVD
尼加拉瓜（Nicaragua）	馬拿瓜（Managua）	MGA
瓜地馬拉（Guatemala）	瓜地馬拉（Guatemala）	GUA
多明尼加（Dominican Republic）	聖多明哥（Santo Domingo）	SDQ
玻利維亞（Bolivia）	拉巴斯（La Paz）	LPB
牙買加（Jamaica）	京士頓（Kingston）	KIN
波多黎各（Puerto）	聖湖安（San Juan）	SJU
海地（Haiti）	太子港（Port au Prince）	PAP
牙買加（Jamaica）	蒙特哥灣（Montego Bay）	MBJ
哥斯大黎加（Costa Rica）	聖約瑟（San Jose）	SJO
宏都拉斯（Honduras）	德古斯加巴（Tegucigalpa）	TGU

墨西哥（Mexico）	亞加普科（Acapucco）	ACA
巴貝多（Barbados）	橋鎮（Bridge Town）	BGI
千里達及托巴哥（Republic of Trinidad and Tobogo）	西班牙港（Port of Spain）	POS
巴拉圭（Paraguay）	亞松森（Asuncion）	ASU
巴西（Brazil）	瑪瑙斯（Manaus）	MAO
巴西（Brazil）	雷雪夫（Recife）	REL
蘇利南共和國（Republic of Suriname）	巴拉馬利波（Paramaribo）	PBM
歐洲地區		
英國（England）	倫敦（London）	LON
英國（England）	愛丁堡（Edinburgh）	EDI
英國（England）	直布羅陀（Gibraltar）	GIB
英國（England）	曼徹斯特（Manchester）	MAN
英國（England）	格拉斯哥（Glasgow）	GLA
法國（France）	巴黎（Paris）	PAR
法國（France）	尼斯（Nice）	NCE
瑞士（Switzerland）	日內瓦（Geneva）	GVA
瑞士（Switzerland）	蘇黎世（Zurich）	ZRH
德國（Germany）	柏林（Berlin）	BER
德國（Germany）	漢堡（Hamberg）	HAM
德國（Germany）	法蘭克福（Frankfurt）	FRA
德國（Germany）	科隆（Cologne）	CGN
德國（Germany）	慕尼黑（Munich）	MUC
德國（Germany）	波昂（Bonn）	BNJ
德國（Germany）	杜塞道夫（Dussdolf）	DUS
德國（Germany）	斯圖加特（Stuttgart）	STR
丹麥（Denmark）	哥本哈根（Copenhagen）	CPH

保加利亞（Bulgaria）	索菲亞（Sofia）	SOF
愛爾蘭（Ireland）	都柏林（Dublin）	DUB）
愛爾蘭（Ireland）	香農（Shannon）	SNN
比利時（Belgium）	布魯塞爾（Brussels）	BRU
波蘭（Poland）	華沙（Warsaw）	WAW
荷蘭（Holland）	阿姆斯特丹（Amsterdam）	AMS
奧地利（Republic of Austria）	維也納（Vienna）	VIE
捷克（Czech Republic）	布拉格（Prague）	PRG
匈牙利（Hungary）	布達佩斯（Budapest）	BUD
希臘（Greece）	雅典（Athens）	ATH
義大利（Italy）	米蘭（Milan）	MIL
義大利（Italy）	羅馬（Rome）	ROM
西班牙（Spain）	巴塞隆納（Barcelona）	BCN
土耳其（Turkey）	伊斯坦堡（Istanbul）	IST
葡萄牙（Portugal）	里斯本（Lisbon）	LIS
西班牙（Spain）	馬德里（Madrid）	MAD
塞爾維亞共和國（Serbia）	貝爾格萊德（Belgrade）	BEG
羅馬尼亞（Romania）	布加勒斯（Bucharest）	BUH
挪威（Norway）	奧斯陸（Oslo）	OSL
瑞典（Sweden）	斯德哥爾摩（Stockholm）	STO
芬蘭（Finland）	赫爾辛基（Helsinki）	HEL
美洲地區		
美國（U.S.A）	紐約（New York）	NYK
美國（U.S.A）	費城（Philadelphia）	PHL
美國（U.S.A）	波士頓（Boston）	BOS
美國（U.S.A）	華盛頓（Washington）	WAS
美國（U.S.A）	底特律（Detroit）	DTT

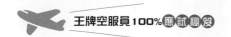
美國（U.S.A）	克里夫蘭（Cleveland）	CLE
美國（U.S.A）	芝加哥（Chicago）	CHI
美國（U.S.A）	匹茲堡（Pittsburgh）	PIT
美國（U.S.A）	水牛城（Buffalo）	BUF
美國（U.S.A）	聖路易（ST. Louis）	STL
美國（U.S.A）	印第安那（Indianapolis）	IND
美國（U.S.A）	明尼亞玻利（Minneapolis）	MSP
美國（U.S.A）	堪薩斯城（Kansas City）	MKC
美國（U.S.A）	休斯頓（Huston）	HOU
美國（U.S.A）	達拉斯（Dalas）	DFW
美國（U.S.A）	亞特蘭大（Atlanta）	ATL
美國（U.S.A）	新奧爾良（New Orleans）	MSY
美國（U.S.A）	奧克拉荷馬城（Oklahoma City）	OKC
美國（U.S.A）	邁阿密（Miami）	MIA
美國（U.S.A）	圖森（Tucson）	TUS
美國（U.S.A）	小岩石城（Little Rock）	LIT
美國（U.S.A）	丹佛（Denver）	DEN
美國（U.S.A）	辛辛那提（Cincinnati）	CVG
美國（U.S.A）	鳳凰城（Phoenix）	PHX
美國（U.S.A）	鹽湖城（Salt Lake City）	SLC
美國（U.S.A）	拉斯維加斯（Las Vegas）	LAS
美國（U.S.A）	舊金山（San Francisco）	SFO
美國（U.S.A）	阿波寇爾喀（Albuoerque）	ABQ
美國（U.S.A）	波特蘭（Portland）	PDX
美國（U.S.A）	洛杉磯（Los Angeles）	LAX
美國（U.S.A）	西雅圖（Seattle）	SEA

美國（U.S.A）	安克拉治（Anchorage）	ANC
美國（U.S.A）	關島（Guam）	GUM
美國（U.S.A）	聖荷西（San Jose）	SJC
美國（U.S.A）	奧蘭多（Orlando）	ORL
美國（U.S.A）	聖荷西（San Jose）	SJC
美國（U.S.A）	聖安東尼（San Antonio）	SAT
美國（U.S.A）	巴爾的摩（Baltimore）	MKE
美國（U.S.A）	米爾瓦基（Milwakee）	MKE
美國（U.S.A）	夏威夷（Honolulu）	HNL
加拿大（Canada）	多倫多（Toronto）	YYZ
加拿大（Canada）	溫哥華（Vancouver）	YVR
加拿大（Canada）	渥太華（Ottawa）	YOW
加拿大（Canada）	蒙特婁（Montreal）	YMQ
加拿大（Canada）	哈立法克斯（Halifax）	YHZ
加拿大（Canada）	干達（Gander）	YQX
加拿大（Canada）	愛德頓（Edmonton）	YEA
加拿大（Canada）	卡加立（Calgary）	YVC
加拿大（Canada）	溫尼伯（Winnipeg）	YMG
中東及非洲地區		
埃及（Egypt）	開羅（Cairo）	CAI
南非（South Africa）	開普敦（Capetown）	CPT
黎巴嫩（Lebanon）	貝魯特（Beirut）	BEY
以色列（Israel）	台拉維夫（Tel Aviv）	TLV
敘利亞（Syria）	大馬士革（Danascus）	DAM
約旦（Jordan）	安曼（Amman）	AMM
沙烏地阿拉伯（Saudi Arabia）	吉達（Jeddah）	JED
巴林王國（Kingdom of Bahrain）	巴林（Bahrain）	BAH

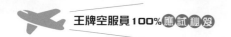
南非（South Africa）	約翰尼斯堡 （Johan Nfaburg）	JNB
剛果（Congo）	金夏沙（Kinshasa）	FIA
馬爾他共和國 （Repubic of Malta）	馬爾他（Malta）	MLA
突尼斯共和國（The Republic of Tunisia）	突尼斯（Tunisia）	TUN
塞內加爾共和國 （Republic of Senegal）	達卡（Dakar）	DKR
模里西斯共和國 （Republic of Mauritius）	模里西斯（Mauritius）	MRU
阿拉伯聯合大公國 （United Arab Emirates）	杜拜（Dubai）	DXB
科威特（Kuwait）	科威特（Kuwait）	KWI
伊拉克（Iraq）	巴格達（Baghdad）	BGW
伊朗（Iran）	德黑蘭（Tehran）	THR
利比亞（Libya）	地黎波斯（Tripoli）	TIP
阿爾及利亞（Democratic and People's Republic of Algeria）	阿爾及爾（Algiers）	ALG
摩洛哥 （Kingdom of Morocco）	卡薩馬達卡 （Casablanca）	CAS
西班牙（Spain）	拉斯馬巴斯 （Laspalmas）	LPA
幾內亞共和國 （Republic of Guinea）	科那克里（Conakry）	CKY
塞拉里昂（Republic of Sierra Leone）	自由城（Free Town）	FNA
馬里（Republic of Mali）	巴馬科（Bamako）	BKO
象牙海岸（Ivory Coast）	阿必尚（Abidjan）	ABJ

賴比瑞亞共和國 （Republic of Liberia）	蒙羅維亞（Monrovia）	MLW
尼日爾共和國 （The Republic of Niger）	尼阿美（Niamey）	NIM
加納 （Republic of Ghana）	阿克拉（Accra）	ACC
布基納法索 （Burkina Faso）	瓦加杜古 （Ouagadougou）	OUA
查德共和國（The Republic of Chad）	拉米堡（Fort Lamy）	FTL
查德共和國（The Republic of Chad）	恩將納（N'Djamena）	NDJ
喀麥隆共和國（Republic of Cameroon）	亞恩德（Yaounde）	YAO
貝寧共和國（The Republic of Benin）	科多努（Cotonou）	COO
奈及利亞（Nigeria）	拉哥斯（Lagos）	LOS
甘比亞（Gambia）	自由府（Libreville）	LVB
安哥拉共和國 （Republic of Angola）	盧安達（Luanda）	LAD
贊比亞（Zambia）	溫黎克（Windhoek）	WDH
贊比亞（Zambia）	露沙卡（Lusaka）	LUN
蘇丹（The Republic of the Sudan）	卡吐穆（Khartoum）	KRT
土耳其（Turkey）	伊斯坦堡（Istanbul）	IST
土耳其（Turkey）	安卡拉（Ankara）	ANK
葉門（Yemen）	亞丁（Aden）	ADE
阿曼（Oman）	馬斯開特（Muscat）	MCT
伊朗（Iran）	阿巴具（Abadan）	ABD

馬達加斯加（Republic of Madagascar）	塔那那次棉（Tananarive）	TNR
尼日利亞（Nigeria）	洛梅（Lome）	LFW
萊索托王國（Kingdom of Lesotho）	馬基魯（Maseru）	MSU
史瓦濟蘭（Swaziland）	馬基尼（Manzini）	MTS
卡塔爾（Qatar）	杜哈（Doha）	DOH
沙特阿拉伯（Kingdom of Saudi Arabia）	利雅德（Riyadh）	RUH
馬拉威共和國（Republic of Malawi）	里郎威（Lilongwe）	LLW
馬拉威共和國（Republic of Malawi）	布蘭太（Blantyre）	BLZ
坦桑尼亞（Tanzania）	達來撒蘭（Dar Es Salaam）	DAR
索馬里（Somalia）	摩加迪修（Mogadishu）	MGO
烏干達共和國（The Republic of Uganda）	恩特比／坎帕拉（Entebbe/Kampala）	EBB
埃塞俄比亞聯邦民主共和國（Federal Democratic Republic of Ethiopia）	阿迪斯阿魯巴（Addis Ababa）	ADD
肯亞共和國（Republic of Kenya）	奈洛彼（Nairobi）	NBO
大洋洲地區		
澳大利亞（Australia）	達爾文（Darwin）	DRW
澳大利亞（Australia）	雪梨（Sydney）	SYD
澳大利亞（Australia）	伯斯（Perth）	PER
澳大利亞（Australia）	凱恩斯（Cairns）	CNS
澳大利亞（Australia）	坎培拉（Canberra）	CBR
澳大利亞（Australia）	基督城（Christchurch）	CHC

澳大利亞（Australia）	布里斯本（Brisbane）	BNE
澳大利亞（Australia）	墨爾本（Melbourne）	MEB
紐西蘭（New Zealand）	威靈頓（Wellington）	WLG
紐西蘭（New Zealand）	奧克蘭（Auckland）	AKL
法屬新喀里多尼亞（New Caledonia）	努美亞（Noumea）	NOU
巴布亞紐幾內亞（Papua New Guinea）	摩勒斯比港（Potr Moresby）	POM
斐濟（Fiji）	蘇瓦（Suba）	SUV
法屬波利尼西亞（French Polynesia）	大溪地（Papeete）	PPT

Learn Smart! 059

王牌空服員 100% 應試秘笈（附 MP3）

作　　　者　蔡靈靈
發 行 人　周瑞德
執行總監　齊心瑀
企劃編輯　陳欣慧
執行編輯　饒美君
校　　對　編輯部
封面構成　高鍾琪

圖片來源　www.shutterstock.com
內頁構成　菩薩蠻數位文化有限公司
印　　製　大亞彩色印刷製版股份有限公司
初　　版　2016 年 6 月
定　　價　新台幣 379 元
出　　版　倍斯特出版事業有限公司
電　　話　(02) 2351-2007
傳　　真　(02) 2351-0887
地　　址　100 台北市中正區福州街 1 號 10 樓之 2
E - m a i l　best.books.service@gmail.com
網　　址　www.bestbookstw.com

港澳地區總經銷　泛華發行代理有限公司
地　　　　址　香港新界將軍澳工業邨駿昌街 7 號 2 樓
電　　　　話　(852) 2798-2323
傳　　　　真　(852) 2796-5471

國家圖書館出版品預行編目資料

王牌空服員 100% 應試秘笈 / 蔡靈靈著.
-- 初版. -- 臺北市 : 倍斯特, 2016.06
　面；　公分. --（Learn smart! ; 59）
ISBN 978-986-92855-2-0（平裝附光碟片）

1. 英語 2. 航空勤務員 3. 讀本

805.18　　　　　　　　105008255

Simply Learning, Simply Best

Simply Learning, Simply Best